# TWISTED DESTINY

## BY: V.E. AVANCE

V.E. Avance
Twisted Destiny

© 2015, Avance
V.E. Avance Publishing
**veavance@gmail.com**

# ACKNOWLEDGMENTS

First, a big shout out to the woman who raised me, Elsie Avance. I love you with all that I am and I know that I wouldn't be who I am without your guidance. I love you more than words can express.

To my husband, thank you for your continued support in all my endeavors.

Shannan Lucckesi, thank you for all your support. I love you like you were my own sister.

To Joyce and Warren Webb, what would I do without you two? I love you like you were my parents and I hope to have many more years with you two.

To my children, you both light up my life beyond words. Without you to pester me daily, I would lose my mind. I love you both with all I have and you are the best things I have ever done. I love you my little ones!

To my street team, The Avancers, you girls are absolutely amazing and I have had the joy of getting to know many of you on a personal and deep level.

To my PA's, Lesa Goodwin and Julie Otis; you girls are amazing. I couldn't have asked for better PA's.

To my editors and friends, Stephanie Kennel and Angela McMasters; you're both amazing. I love you girls!

To my fans, thank you for supporting me and buying my work. An author is only as successful as their team and fans. Without your support, well there would be no V.E. Avance.

And last but not least, thank you to all the bloggers and beta readers. I hope to meet all of you during my signings in the next few years.

# TABLE OF CONTENT

| | |
|---|---|
| One | 1 |
| Two | 12 |
| Three | 19 |
| Four | 26 |
| Five | 35 |
| Six | 40 |
| Seven | 50 |
| Eight | 57 |
| Nine | 63 |
| Ten | 69 |
| Eleven | 75 |
| Twelve | 82 |
| Thirteen | 89 |
| Fourteen | 94 |
| Fifteen | 108 |
| Sixteen | 116 |
| Seventeen | 124 |
| Eighteen | 131 |
| Nineteen | 137 |
| Twenty | 143 |
| Twenty One | 147 |
| Twenty Two | 151 |
| Twenty Three | 156 |
| Twenty Four | 161 |
| Twenty Five | 164 |
| Twenty Six | 169 |
| Twenty Seven | 178 |
| Twenty Eight | 183 |
| Twenty Nine | 187 |
| Thirty | 191 |
| Thirty One | 197 |
| Thirty Two | 202 |
| Thirty Three | 206 |
| Thirty Four | 213 |

Epilogue                                     222
Author's Note                                226

# CHAPTER ONE

## **August 2011**

"God damn it!" Chris hollers when his tractor quit working clear across the field from the machine shed. Since inheriting his family's farm a few months ago, he's had nothing but issues with the equipment. "How the hell did my father do this as long as he did?" Chris hops off the tractor and begins the forty-five minute walk back.

Chris is still fuming when his fifteen year old son, Charles, drives up along the dirt road between the house and the field. "Hey Dad, Mom noticed the tractor hadn't moved in a while and thought that you may need some help," Charles scoots across the bench seat of the old, run-down Ford.

"Thanks, Son," Chris positions himself behind the steering wheel. "That damn tractor crapped out on me again and of course, your father being a dingbat and all, I forgot to put the tool box in the tractor before leaving this morning."

"Ah, Dad, you're not a dingbat. You've been away from this type of work for how long now?"

Chris thinks back to the last time he stepped foot on this land before coming back to take it over when his parents passed away. It was a cool December day in 1995; snow littered the Nebraska countryside. Laura's cries of agony pierced through his body, straight to his heart, but his father wouldn't allow him to step foot near her. *I don't understand why I can't comfort her,* he thought to himself.

"Dad, are you still with me?" Charles calls out to him. He's still next to his son in the old beat up Ford but his mind was a million miles away.

"Yes, Charlie, I was just thinking about the last time I was here on this farm. You were barely a newborn the day I left Greenwich and I never looked back." Chris turns the truck around and heads back to the farmhouse, trying to push the memory out of his mind.

\*\*\*

# Avance

Scarlet Haggis is standing at the kitchen sink cleaning up the last of the pots used to make that night's supper. Chris had broken down, again, and Charlie, their eldest son, went out to rescue him from the long and dusty walk home. The youngest girls, Audrey and Suzanne, have been nagging and complaining for supper. Seeing as Chris and Charlie might not be back for a while, she reasoned that it was best to feed the younger three kids, even though James wasn't really complaining like his younger sisters were. Scarlet decided to eat supper with the younger kids and allow Charlie and Chris to dine together.

Many nights since moving to the farm in Greenwich Scarlet has dreamt of her life, their life, back in Los Angeles. She was a paralegal for a prominent lawyer and Chris was a CEO at an up-and-coming financial institution. Their home was beautiful, their children attended prestigious private schools and they took vacations twice a year. Scarlet will never forget the day her life was flipped upside down. One call and everything changed.

## **May 2011**

*"Ok guys, go wash your faces and hands and brush your teeth," Scarlet told her four children; Charles, James, Audrey and Suzanne.*

*Weeknights were always hectic in the Haggis household and that Thursday night was no exception. Chris was late getting off work and Scarlet was running around trying to pick kids up and drop them off for their extracurricular activities. Dinner, again, was an hour late which meant the kids' bedtime would be an hour late as well. I just want, for once, to have enough time to relax in a bubble bath, Scarlet thought to herself as she began to clear the table.*

*"Have I told you how much I love you?" Chris wrapped his arms around Scarlet's waist and planted kisses up her neck before catching her earlobe, gently, between his teeth. Scarlet squeals and twists her head into her shoulder, breaking the connection of Chris' mouth on her ear.*

*Scarlet ran her hands up Chris' chest and circled them around his neck. "You always tell me you love me, but you show it to me more than anything," she kissed his lips.*

*The kids came screaming into the room and the phone began to ring. "Just another night in the Haggis home," Scarlet smiled before rounding the children back upstairs while Chris turned to answer the phone.*

*Once the children were placed in their pajamas and everyone was snuggled down for the night, Scarlet made her way back downstairs to enjoy a few moments of silence with her husband before they retired to bed.*

*When she made her way into the living room, she could tell something wasn't quite right about Chris. He was sitting on the loveseat staring at a blank television screen with a glass of whisky in his hand. "Chris, what's wrong?" She took the vacant seat next to him and held his free hand in hers.*

*"They're both dead," he stated, matter-of-factly.*

*Confusion spread across Scarlet's face. "Dead—who?" she questioned, squeezing his hand.*

*"Mom and Dad—they were both found murdered this evening," Chris swirled the amber colored liquid in his glass. "The neighbor hadn't seen Dad working the field today and became so concerned that he went to the farm house and discovered their bodies."*

*Scarlet's mouth dropped open as her brain began to search for the right words. Murdered? How can that be? No one gets murdered in Greenwich, Nebraska. As she regained her composure, Chris began to speak again.*

*"We need to fly out this weekend. I have some things to take care of since I'm the only living next of kin. I have to plan their funerals and*

*figure out what to do with the old farm house,"
he said, more to himself instead of his wife.*

*Scarlet's mind was going a mile a minute.
Funeral, travel arrangement for a family of six
last minute, informing schools and jobs of family
emergency—I need to make a list of everything
that needs to be done so I don't forget anything
important.  "Did the Sheriff explain what
happened to your parents?" Scarlet quizzed
Chris, curiosity getting the best of her.*

*"Yeah, it was gruesome," he trailed off, his eyes
misted over.  After a few silent moments Chris
began again.  "Mom was found in the kitchen.
Apparently, the killer surprised her while she
was pouring coffee.  It appears that he cut her
throat from ear to ear.  The Sheriff says she bled
out quickly and probably wasn't even aware of
what was happening."*

*Scarlet gasped in horror of how her mother-in-
law was killed.  To slit someone's throat, from
ear-to-ear, is personal.  Who would do such a
thing?*

*"Dad was found in their bedroom.  It looked as if
he were just finishing getting ready to start his
day.  He was shot through both knee caps and
then stabbed multiple times.  We won't know
how many times, exactly, until the medical
examiner finishes the autopsy, but the Sheriff
knows that there were more than a dozen*

*wounds to his chest and abdomen," he takes a long swig of whisky. The burning of the liquid down his throat caused him to shutter. Chris was not a drinker, usually, but, apparently, today was as good a day as any to let the alcohol take control.*

*"It gets worse, Scarlet," Chris continued. "Mom was sexually assaulted by the killer. They believe that he made his way back into the kitchen where he raped her corpse," he said with anger radiating in his face. "What sane person fucks a corpse?" he raised his voice, the whiskey glass shattered against the wall and reminisces of the amber colored drink littered the floor.*

*Scarlet, unsure of what to do, twisted her fingers around the hem of her shirt. She'd been married to Chris for more than a decade and had never heard him raise his voice, not even when the kids were running amuck through the house or when Charlie was suspended from school for three days for a fight with the neighborhood bully. This was uncharted ground for her.*

*"I'm sorry, baby, I didn't mean to lose my temper," Chris said as he sits next to his wife and placed his hands on either side of her face. He kissed her gently on her forehead, "I'm so sorry. You don't deserve to witness my anger."*

# Twisted Destiny

*"Chris, you don't have any reason to be sorry. You just heard some devastating and disturbing news. Your reaction is normal," Scarlet tried to reassure him. She kissed the tip of his nose. "Why don't I start booking flights and making a list of things that need to be done while you…well, while you clean up your mess and pour yourself another drink?"*

✷✷✷

*"Hey honey," Chris' voice pulls Scarlet out of the past and back to the future. "Sorry I'm late for supper. That damned tractor broke down again and, you know me, I forgot to grab the tool box before I headed out this afternoon," he shrugs his shoulders and plants a kiss on her cheek. "I'm going to wash up. I'll be back in a few for supper," Chris heads to the half-bath located off the family room.*

*Scarlet pulls Chris and Charlie's plates from the oven where she was keeping them warm and places them on the breakfast nook. Charlie washes up at the kitchen sink before taking his seat at the nook just as his mom is pouring his and his dad's glasses of sweet tea.*

*"Thank you Mom," he gives her his innocent smile while waiting for his dad to join him.*

*"You're welcome, Charlie."*

# Avance

Chris comes dragging in a few moments later. "Oh my, this looks delicious," he says as he sits and begins to eat.

Scarlet sits next to Chris. "How long do you think that old tractor is going to last?"

"Oh, that old tractor still has a lot of life in it. Tractors, both new and old, break down all the time. It's cheaper to continue to fix them than it is to run out and buy a new one," Chris explains in between bites.

"Chris," she sighs, "I want to go back to Los Angeles. I get bored here all day and I miss working. I loved my job and the life we created, together, back home."

Chris runs his hand through his hair, "I know you want to move back home but this house is my home. It's been in my family for more than a hundred years and there is no one else to take over the farm," Chris explains for the umpteenth time. "Look, I know you miss work. Why don't you find a job in town? The kids will be back in school next week and Charlie is old enough and responsible enough to help care for the younger kids until you get home," Chris suggests to her.

Charlie looks over from his dinner and gives his mom a smile. "I wouldn't mind helping with the kids."

*"Thank you, Charlie. You really are a good boy," she forces a smile, not at her son but at the situation.*

*"I know that I can go to work but I miss the life we had in LA. It's so slow here and things are radically different and I don't like it," she turns back to Chris.*

*"Scarlet, I don't know what to tell you. Life here is better, if you'd just stop thinking about what you're losing and look at what you're gaining. Crime rates are almost non-existent, there is no smog and no traffic jams."*

*"Yeah, there's no crime except for the double homicide that took place right in this very home," she spats while standing and heading upstairs to their bedroom—the room that her father-in-law was murdered in.*

*"Damn it," Chris mutters under his breath as he rises and places his empty plate in the sink. Scarlet doesn't understand that murder—what happened to his parents, is a rare thing to happen in Greenwich. Murder happens every day in Los Angeles. He just wishes that she could see Greenwich through his eyes.*

*"It's okay Dad. She just needs some time. It's a big change coming from a bustling city to an easy living county town.*

# Avance

*"You're wise beyond your years.  Now, go get yourself ready for bed.  I think we have a busy day ahead of ourselves tomorrow."*

*Charlie heads upstairs for a quick shower before bed, leaving Chris alone downstairs to think of the past, present and future.*

*"You better wash your dirty dishes," Scarlet hollers down the stairwell.*

*Chris rolls his eyes and soaps up the dish cloth and begins washing the six items used for his and Charlie's supper.  He doesn't really want to be in this farm house, not for the same reason as Scarlet.  The only reason he can't just sell this land is because of her.  The last memory he had of her was in this home—on this land.*

# CHAPTER TWO

The wind whipped Laura's dress and muddled her long brown hair. She was absolutely gorgeous. Chris had known her all her life but he had never observed her true beauty. Her beautiful hazel eyes glistened in the moonlight. A twitching in his trousers alerted him to how deep his feelings were for Laura. He placed his hand upon her face and wrapped his other arm around her waist. No words were said but their desire spoke louder than words. He leaned down and kissed her soft lips. The kiss was incredible and his desire for her was becoming unbearable. He needed to be with her just as much as he needed his next breath. He laid her back on a stack of loose hay in the family barn while he entwined his fingers into her hair.

A soft moan escaped from Laura. Chris ran his free hand up her thigh and to her hips. Laura's back arched with the same desire and anticipation. The kiss deepened between them. A soft moan escaped again but this time, Chris muffled it with a heated kiss.

The alarm buzzes and Chris is pulled out of the dream that has plagued him since moving back to his family home. He glances at the clock and sees that it's a quarter after four in the morning. He tosses the covers back and makes his way to the bathroom. Laura had not crossed his mind in more than a decade and he preferred it that way. Their love—relationship, was not right. It was a sin –an abomination. A few hours after his parents discovered their relationship, Chris was sent away. He never returned, not even for Laura's funeral a mere six months later.

He splashes water over his face in hopes of washing away her memory. He needs to get out there and get that tractor fixed this morning so that he can finish preparing the ground to sow lettuce seeds. This is the final week to plant lettuce if he plans on having them harvested before the first snowfall of the year.

A knock pulls him from his thoughts. "Dad, I need to use the restroom," the voice of his oldest son, Charlie, softly echoes through the bathroom.

"Ok son, I'm almost done. Give me a few minutes," Chris brushes his hair with one hand and his teeth with the other. Once he's done, he opens the bathroom door to see Charlie standing there, dressed for the day and doing the potty dance—dancing from one foot to another. "What are you doing up so early?"

"I want to help you, Dad," Charlie pushes past his dad and closes the bathroom door.

Chris and Charlie head out to the field where they left the tractor last night. Chris has a toolbox in hand and Charlie is bursting with excitement about working with his dad. Living in California, Charlie didn't get to spend a lot of time with his father. "I'm excited about working on this fine piece of machinery," Charlie says to his dad when they approach the tractor.

"You like working with your hands, son?"

"Yes, I do. I never got a chance to do any manual labor in Los Angeles," Charlie points out.

"Well, they have FFA and welding and mechanic classes at the local high school. Maybe you should sign up for those classes when you start school next week."

"Really?" excitement courses through his veins. "I think that I'd really enjoy that. That prep school you and Mom enrolled me in limited my exposure to what I really enjoy."

"Well, son, that was primarily your mother's doing and she only did it with the best of intentions. She wanted to give you and your siblings the best opportunities in life."

"I know. I'm not mad. I'm just happy that I finally get to do what I enjoy."

They continue to tinker with the tractor while making mindless chit chat. The tractor is up and working just before lunchtime. Charlie and Chris head back to the house for a quick bite before finishing preparing the land.

He stalks the farm house and its new occupants. He's been lurking in the woods surrounding the farm for the past six months. He stalked the perimeter of the property for six weeks before he started braving his way onto the land and around the dwelling. The intention was never to kill the old couple. He went to talk to them the night before. He was unprepared for their irrational response to his unannounced visit.

He couldn't allow the couple to tell anyone about him and what he was looking for. No way! If word got out, how would people look at him? Nope, he couldn't allow that to happen. He made his way back to his shack where he grabbed his hunting knife and his small caliber revolver, both of which he had stolen.

In the early morning hours before the sun began to rise, he made his way back to the couples' house. He waited in the cover of darkness for morning to break. At four o'clock in the morning, he saw a light turn on in the upstairs bedroom and one in the kitchen. Now was the time to pounce. He crept up to the house. No one locks their doors here, so he opened the back door and made his way in. His first target—the woman. She would be the easiest one to take out. As quietly as possible, he tip toed behind her. He wrapped one arm around her waist and with the other, he sliced her throat from ear to ear with the hunting knife. He laid her on the floor as soundlessly as possible and made sure his face was the last one she ever saw before she bled out.

As soon as he knew she was no longer alive, he made his way up the stairs. The old stairs creaked with his weight. He could still hear the shower running, so he knew he didn't need to be too quiet. He lurked in the bedroom, waiting for the old man to come back in the room. It wasn't a long wait, but the excitement was overwhelming. In the beginning, he didn't think he could stomach taking a life, but the adrenaline rush he got from this act was invigorating.

The old man made his way back to the bedroom. Before he had time to react to the trespasser in his room, he fired the first shot to his right knee cap. The scream that came from the old man was ear piercing—thrilling even. The next shot, hitting the left knee cap, didn't cause as much of an earsplitting scream as the first, but it was still exhilarating.

"Why are you doing this?" the old man pleaded with him, but he just laughed an evil laugh as he pulled out the hunting knife and casually walked toward him. "Please, I'm begging you!" He was pleading for his life.

His lips turn up as he raised the knife above his head. "You should've never called me an abomination," he said before bringing the knife down into the old man's chest. He moaned with pleasure as the old man moaned in despair. "You should have accepted me as I am." Another strike to the old man's chest made him smile.

It wasn't long before the old man took his final breath. Just to be sure he was really dead, he stabbed him several more times. As he walked back down the stairs, blood dripping from the hunting knife, he decided he couldn't leave without taking a little something.

He made his way back to the kitchen where the old lady was lying. He lifted up her dress as he dropped his pants. He moaned with twisted pleasure as he raped the woman—unable to say no or defend herself. After he completed the act, he zipped himself up and strolled out the front door.

A smile creeps along his face at the memory of killing the elderly couple. He now sits in the woods again staring at the old farm house watching as each light shuts off, one by one. *It won't be much longer now*.

# CHAPTER THREE

Laura's body looked exquisite standing before Chris in nothing but a bra and pair of panties. Her soft brown hair laid flat across her back and she looked up at Chris through hooded eyes. She was nervous and a little embarrassed. "You look absolutely stunning," the young seventeen year old said to her. Her cheeks blushed as her eyes darted down. "Hey, look at me," Chris said as he stepped toward her and took her chin in his hand. "You are gorgeous, Laura," his lips brushed against hers.

Chris wrapped one hand around Laura's waist while the other traveled under her panties. A moan escaped her throat as she wrapped her arms around his neck and leaned her head back in pure ecstasy.

Chris jolts awake, sweat pouring down his face and heart pounding. Another dream or nightmare, depending, on how one looked at it, plagued him for yet another night. The thought of Laura sends chills down Chris' spine. She was his first love, but their love couldn't be. He had to end their relationship, though it wasn't easy and he spent many nights thinking about her and dreaming about her. His parents didn't understand the love they felt between each other and made sure that they would never be together again.

Chris shakes Laura's image from his head as he climbs out of bed. Though he loves being back on the farm, he still hates waking up early. A farmer starts working before the sun comes up and doesn't end his day until well after the sun has set. Scarlet tries to be a good wife of a farmer but most mornings she won't roll out of bed before he heads out for the day so he is on his own for breakfast. After toasting an English muffin, he sits down to eat his minute amount of breakfast and indulges in his steaming cup of coffee.

"Hey Dad," Charlie rubs his eyes as he walks to the toaster to pop in an English muffin himself.

"Do you mind if I head out with you again today?"

Charlie and Chris have always had a special bond. Though Chris loves his other children—James, Audrey and Suzanne, the bond that he and Charlie share is greater than that of the bonds of his younger three children. "Sure son, we have a busy day today. We have to get the crops planted if we plan on having them ready for harvesting on time."

"Well, two bodies are better than one and, together, we will get it done quicker," Charlie sits next to his dad to eat his breakfast. When the family first moved to Nebraska, Charlie was the only one who was open-minded about the move. While his mom and siblings were moaning and groaning about the move and making his dad's life a living hell, Charlie embraced the idea and the change in scenery.

As Charlie and Chris begin their long day, they're unaware of the pair of eyes that are stalking their every move. They're unaware of the thoughts that plague their demented stalker. He doesn't want to hurt Chris and Charlie, but the rest of them must go. They're the true abomination. Though watching their blood drip from his knife and witnessing them take their final breath brings a smile to his face, he has no intentions of murdering the remaining six Haggis family members so long as they get the message.

Being bounced from one group home to another wasn't the family that he longed for. He wanted a mother to hold him when he was scared and a father to teach him how to play baseball. He wanted a brother to play with and even to pick on a little. He could've had all that had things worked out the way nature had intended. Instead of a family, he ended up with a dead mother and no idea who his father was—until now.

Scarlet stretches her arms above her head as the sunlight spreads over her face. The sound of the birds singing outside the bedroom window is the only thing that she loves about living on the farm. She and Chris have been married for almost fourteen years and she has known something life changing happened to Chris here right after the birth of Charlie but he never spoke of it. Chris' willingness to move back to the home he tried for years to escape from boggled her mind.

She remembers the day that she met Chris like it was yesterday. She was working at Procter and Sampson as a paralegal when Chris came through the front door into the waiting room carrying an infant in a car seat. Her heart skipped a beat and she couldn't help but take another look at the man standing before her. Chris was tall, taller than the average man. His brown hair accented his emerald eyes. Scarlet, somehow, regained her composure, "I'm Scarlet Stanley. Can I help you sir?" she asks as she walked over and extended her hand.

Chris switched the infant seat from his right hand to the left and returned the gesture. "Hi, I'm Chris Haggis and I hope you can help me. I'm looking for a Mr. Procter. I have an appointment at two o'clock." His eyes glisten in the sunlight and Scarlet is unable to contain the smile that spreads across her face. He was much more handsome up-close.

"His secretary didn't call you? Mr. Procter had a family emergency this afternoon and needed to push his appointments to another day." Scarlet tries to keep her voice steady. Chris makes her insides feel like a teenage girl who has a crush on the quarterback.

With a depressing look on his face, he shook his head as the baby in the portable seat began to squirm. "I was not informed of his absence."

Scarlet feels sorry for him. The happy and beautiful man before her morphed into a sad and depressed man. She quickly thinks of the other attorney at the firm. "Mr. Sampson is in and, last I checked, was available. I can go find out if he has time to meet with you today."

"That would be great," he replied as he put the car seat down and pulled out a bottle from the diaper bag draped over his shoulder. "I just need to get this matter taken care of so I can get home and take care of this little guy."

"He's a cutie. I'll be right back," she turned and went in search of Mr. Sampson. Procter and Sampson specialize in custody and family law. As quickly as she parted from the waiting room, she returned. "Mr. Sampson said he can see you now. Would you mind if I looked after your son while you meet with him?" she offered, cooing at the beautiful baby looking back at her.

Chris looked between the beautiful woman sitting before him and his newborn son. "If it wouldn't be an inconvenience to you, I would appreciate it," he handed the baby boy over to Scarlet. "His name is Charles—Charlie for short. He's just been fed and changed so you shouldn't have any issues with him." Chris walks into the office and the door closes.

It was, at that moment, that she felt a bond with the newborn baby left in her care. Not only did she feel a bond with this baby but, over time, she developed a bond with his father. They dated for a very short time before running to

Vegas and getting married.  And, as the saying goes, the rest is history.

# CHAPTER FOUR

The new school year has finally approached. Scarlet wakes earlier than normal to start getting the kids ready for school—this is the first time that they will ride a bus to school. Suzanne and Audrey jump out of bed ready to go. "We get to ride a big yellow bus!" they scream, jumping all over their beds.

"Yes, you get to ride a big yellow bus but you'll miss the bus if you don't stop jumping around like little jumping beans and get dressed," she pulls each girl off their beds and strips them of their night clothes and wrestles them into their school outfits. "Now, make your beds while I start breakfast."

# Avance

Scarlet knocks on James' and Charlie's doors before heading downstairs. "Time to wake up."

In the kitchen, she scrambles some eggs while bacon sizzles in the skillet. She places bread in the toaster and pours the eggs in another skillet. Just as she's beating the eggs in the skillet the back door flies open. Her head whips in the direction of the sound, her heart skipping a beat. Her eyes meet with her eldest son, "oh, it's just you," she breathes a sigh of relief.

"Sorry Mom. I didn't mean to startle you," Charlie crosses the kitchen and gives his mother a kiss on her cheek.

"What are you doing up so early?"

"Ah, I just wanted to give Dad a hand before I had to get ready for school. I'm going to run upstairs and grab a quick shower. I'll be down in time for breakfast and to walk the kids to the bus stop."

Scarlet gets breakfast on the table and the girls ready for school just in the nick of time. Charlie grabs each girl's hand and James follows alongside Suzanne as her four blessings head out for the quarter mile walk to the bus stop. *Those girls are going to be tired by the time they get home. Waking at half past five is abnormal for them,* she thinks as she begins to clear the breakfast dishes and fill the sink with warm, soapy water. "I wish Chris would install a dishwasher so I'm not spending half my day washing dishes," she mutters to herself.

Scarlet begins her morning chores; making beds, vacuuming, dusting and mopping. She turns her stereo up and lip syncs to her favorite Journey song. She is unable to help but sing when the music starts. *Don't stop believin', hold on to that feeeeelin'...* Scarlet can't carry a tune in a bucket but she doesn't care. Journey has always been her favorite band and she can't help but sing off key and dance like a drunk person. In record time, her chores are done.

The clock above the mantel reads fifteen after nine. *What the hell am I supposed to do now?* Not knowing what to do, she grabs a book from the shelf that she had ordered before leaving Los Angeles. *Hmm, an erotic romance book from Lana Elli. Mommy porn!* She snuggles on the couch and begins to read the first chapter.

*I just finished another six hour...*

The house phone rings, causing her to sigh and place the book on the coffee table in front of her. She rises and makes her way to the kitchen, where the phone is plugged in. "Hello, Haggis residence?"

"You aren't a Haggis. You don't belong there. You need to leave. Leave now, or be sorry later. You don't want to end up like the old couple, do you?" the voice booms out before the line goes dead.

*W-what the fuck? Who the hell was that? Fuck who it is, I'm getting the hell out of here.* Scarlet runs upstairs and begins packing her things. *I need to book a flight for a family of six, look for a place to rent, and try to get our jobs back. What else do I need to do?*

Scarlet's heart is racing. She knows that she's making a mountain out of a mole hill but after her in-laws were viciously murdered in this house, it doesn't take much to cause her to over react. Honestly, they never even caught the party responsible for the murders and now the phone call!

Scarlet is deep in her own thoughts when she hears a voice behind her. "What are you doing?" the voice makes her practically jump out of her skin.

She turns and is face to face with her husband. "Chris, we need to get out of here. I think we can be out by night fall if you help me pack and we can get a redeye flight back to Los Angeles."

"Whoa whoa whoa, what the hell is going on? We're not going anywhere," he walks across the room and sits on the bed. "Come, sit so we can talk about this," he pats the bed next to him.

Scarlet sits down and the fear and stress she's been harboring in her soul for the past two hours rises to the surface in the form of a loud sob. "I-I received a phone call earlier telling me that I'm not a Haggis and I needed to leave before I ended up li...like your parents," wails of fear and sorrow fill the bedroom. The same room her father-in-law was murdered in.

Chris wraps his arms around his shaking wife. *Who in the hell would play this sort of sick joke? That's all this is—a sick and twisted joke from some bored low-life with nothing better to do.* "Honey, it was probably some sort of sick joke. You know, this town is small and everyone knows everyone and everyone knows everyone else's business. These sorts of shenanigans are expected around these parts. We're not in California anymore," Chris tries to comfort his anxiety-ridden wife.

Her sobs begin to dissipate as she pulls away from Chris. "Now don't give me that bullshit. These sorts of things are not expected, at least not by my standards. When people begin to threaten my life, that's where I draw the line. I want to go home and I want to go home now!" Her face reddens with anger—anger toward Chris and this farm and this stupid ass town.

Firmly and very blunt, Chris responds to his wife's outburst. "You are home. This is our home. This is where our children will be raised.

# Avance

It's a great town and the best place to raise our children.  No gangs or violence to corrupt them and good solid work to keep them busy."

"Our home?  OUR HOME?!  Chris, up until your parents were savagely murdered, you never spoke of this place.  Every time I brought up your childhood, you would change the subject.  If it was so bad that you didn't want to speak of it then, why do you want to raise our children here now, in a place you ran from?"  Scarlet tries to understand her husband and why this place is of importance now when it hasn't been for over fifteen years.

Chris runs his fingers through his brown hair and lets out a deep sigh as he sits on the bed.  "There was a falling out between my parents and I right after Charlie was born.  I grabbed my son and left that night.  I wish I didn't have to leave but there was nothing else for me.  I was no longer welcome here."

Scarlet scoots herself next to her husband and kisses his cheek.  "Why?  What happened so many years ago that your parents would disown you?"

"I don't want to talk about it, Scarlet.  Rehashing the past won't undo it.  Just trust me that it was something we couldn't have ever worked out," he replies as he rises from the bed and exits the room.

Scarlet sits there, for a long moment, before busying herself with unpacking the clothes she just minutes ago hastily tossed in her oversized suitcase. *Maybe Chris is right. Maybe it's just some idiot from town messing with them because he has nothing better to do with his life. But, maybe he's wrong. Oh God, what if he's wrong?*

Since it was the kids' first day of school, there was no homework to complete so all the kids dressed in their play clothes and busied themselves around the property. Charlie helped his dad in the field and James built a battle with his army men. Suzanne and Audrey played house out in the play house that Chris built them just days after moving there. Everyone was busy and carefree—everyone but Scarlet.

She just couldn't get that phone call out of her mind. The more she tried to busy herself around the house, the more that phone call crept into the forefront of her mind. She was too busy thinking about the call that she ended up ruining her first dinner ever. "Shit," she screeches as she grabs some flour from the canister and pours over the top of the skillet that burst into flames. "There goes our dinner for the night," she sighs as she begins to cool off and throw away the burnt and flour drenched pork chops that she had been frying for her family.

# Avance

As she's cleaning the mess up, she hears sizzling back at the stove and turns in that direction. "God dammit!" she screams as she rushes to the stove to turn the flame off under the pot of boiling potatoes. Water not only boiled over the pot and on the stove but poured out onto her clean kitchen floor. She sits at the nook and cries—sobs. *That phone call is disrupting my life. I'm going to end up burning down the house! I just want to go home!*

"Honey, are you alright?" Chris places his hand on her shoulder, startling her. She was so caught up in her own thoughts she didn't hear her family come running in the house. She runs her fingers through her hair and rises from the stool to clean up the mess she made in the kitchen.

"I'm fine," she lies. "I just let my mind wander and ruined dinner," she explains as she begins to wipe up the mess from the floor.

"Honey, it's okay. How about we get cleaned up and head into town and eat at the café there? I haven't been there in years and, last time I was there, they served the best chicken fried steak ever," Chris smiles and wiggles his eyebrows.

Scarlet nods her head as Chris disappears upstairs to take a shower and dress for supper. She finishes cleaning the kitchen floor up before heading upstairs to sponge bathe the girls and get them dressed in clean attire for a public dinner. *I just need to get out of the house and clear my head.*

Scarlet's mood had improved by the time the family piled into their car and drove the twenty miles into town. By the time they got to town, ate and drove back, she figured she would be as good as new.

# CHAPTER FIVE

Chris' belly was so full from his chicken fried steak that he had a tough time getting that slice of apple pie down. However, the pie was just as delicious as the chicken fried steak and he couldn't pass it over. Now, as his tummy grumbles and aches, he fully regrets his decision. "Maybe I should have passed on dessert," he mutters as they turn down the dirt road leading to the farmhouse.

Scarlet chuckles her beautiful laugh and concurs with him. *He always overeats, gets sick, swears he's never going to do it again and then does it the next chance he gets.* "If you passed up homemade apple pie, I would have rushed you to the emergency room because that is so not you!" she grins as she takes his hand in hers.

They park the car in front of the house and all begin to pile out. Audrey and Suzanne had fallen asleep so Charlie lifted Audrey from her booster seat to carry her to her bed while Chris grabbed Suzanne. Scarlet walked ahead of them to unlock the door with James dragging his feet behind the group. Scarlet inserts the key into the lock and turns.

No one was prepared for what awaited them on the other side of that locked door. Scarlet gasped, Chris' face turned red with anger, Charlie was startled and James was confused. "What happened, Mommy?" James questions as he looks around the house.

Books that once lined the bookshelf are now littered across the living room floor. All their family photos that once were displayed on the walls are shattered into a gazillion pieces throughout the living room and hallway. Every dish they own is shattered in the kitchen. "I don't know baby," is the only sentence that Scarlet could form.

Chris, after recollecting his thoughts, turns to Scarlet. "You need to get outside with the kids. I'm going to search the house."

Chris searches the house only to discover that the mess is contained to the lower section. He goes back down and retrieves his family. "It's all good guys. Damage is only on the first floor. Let's get the girls to bed and clean up the mess."

Chris grabs Suzanne while Charlie caries up Audrey. They don't even worry about putting pajamas on the girls. They remove their shoes and tuck them in.

Scarlet makes her way upstairs to get James settled for the night while Chris and Charlie make their way back down. "Dad, who do you think would do something like this?" Charlie asks as he looks around the room. The phone has been smashed on the counter and the kitchen and living room are in shambles.

"Son, I don't know. I do know that we need to phone the police but that's sort of out of the question," he shakes head while looking at the destroyed phone. If the cell phones that they had in Los Angeles had service, he could call the police.

"Well, there's no use crying over spilled milk," Charlie says while grabbing a broom and dust pan to begin cleaning up the broken glass.

"Oh honey, let me. I don't want you to cut yourself," Scarlet says as she comes down from the second floor. "Why don't you go straighten up the books in the living room and I'll clean this up," she motions toward the most damaged room in the house.

"Mom, I'm not a baby. I won't cut myself," Charlie says, rolling his eyes but succumbing to his mother's wishes.

"I know you're not a baby but you're my baby," Scarlet responds while pinching Charlie's cheek. The fear is almost overwhelming her but she tries to hide it in front of her children, no matter how old they may be.

"Aww, come on, Mom. I hate my cheeks being pinched," Charlie whines, but flashes his mom a smile.

With the help of Charlie, Scarlet and Chris have the house back in order in no time and are upstairs getting ready for bed. "I'll run into town tomorrow and grab a new phone and some dishes," Scarlet say as she rubs the lotion on her hands.

"That sounds good. And why don't you grab some more picture frames while you're in town?" Chris climbs into bed with a grunt as his joints begin to pop.

"I love you honey and I'm sorry this is happening. I'll stop it one way or another," Chris says, giving Scarlet a kiss on her cheek.

Scarlet has nothing to say to Chris. She told him she wanted to go back to Los Angeles and he doesn't seem to care about what she wants or what's best for the kids. In order to keep her marriage together, she has decided to keep her opinions to herself.

Chris rolls over and turns the light off. Within minutes, he is peacefully snoring next to her while she is wide awake, keeping an ear out for any strange noises. *A dog would be nice—a retriever or Labrador to keep an ear out for any intruder. Since Chris won't move back to Los Angeles, maybe he'll go for a dog if he knows it will help me feel safe.* Scarlet finally drifts off to sleep, hoping she can convince Chris to get the family a puppy in the morning.

# CHAPTER SIX

Laura was in the garden tending to the vegetables while Chris was plowing the fields. Summers in Greenwich were always so beautiful but never as gorgeous as Laura. As Chris admired Laura, he couldn't help but notice that her midsection was beginning to protrude a bit. Her once flat stomach was now poofy. *Maybe she's been eating more since their nightly escapades in the barn,* Chris thinks to himself. He is worn out more now that he and Laura have been exercising together—in unison.

It doesn't matter how big or small Laura is, nothing could make her anything but beautiful.

# Avance

Chris longs to have their relationship in the open but he knows that his parents, let alone the world, would accept it, so for now, their love never leaves the four walls of his family barn.

Chris awakens to Scarlet rubbing against the trouser tent the dream of Laura brought on. "Hey whoa," Chris says, a little startled by her actions. "What are you doing?"

Scarlet stops the motion and looks up at Chris— confused and disoriented. "Well, I was..." she trails off, rolling over. She sits up and slides her feet into her slippers before reaching for her robe. "I'm going to go start breakfast," she mumbles before rising out of bed.

"Scarlet, wait...I didn't mean it in a bad way. I was just startled because you never...or you haven't done that since before we got here. That's all. I didn't mean any offense by it," Chris tries to apologize but Scarlet is in one of her irrational moments. "Damn it," Chris sighs as Scarlet exits the room, shutting the door behind her.

Chris climbs out of bed and begins his morning routine. He changes from his nightwear into his work clothes. He goes into the bathroom and brushes his teeth and combs his brown hair back. *Damn, I'm thinning on the top of my head. When the hell did that happen?* He thinks to himself before laying the comb back on the counter and washing his face.

The smell of bacon hits Chris' nose before the sound of it sizzling in the skillet reaches him. His stomach growls and grumbles as he makes his way out of the bathroom and down the hall. He makes it to the kitchen in record time. "Hey babe," Chris leans in and kisses Scarlet's cheek. "It sure does smell good in here."

"Thank you," Scarlet smiles sheepishly as she turns the pieces of bacon over in the hot pan. "I'm going to make you biscuits and gravy with bacon before you start your long day."

"Yum, I can't wait. But honey, what is this all about?" Chris questions, pointing at the food on the stove.

"I don't know. I guess I was just trying to make up for the past few days. It's been rough and I've not made it any easier by wanting to move back to Los Angeles and I thought I would make it up to you with a hearty breakfast to start your day."

"Well, if I get treated like this every time you have an irrational...er um, bad day, then you can continue to bring them on," he responds with a huge grin that spreads along his face.

"I'm glad you approve," she places his plate in front of him. "Now be careful. It's piping hot."

# Avance

The two eat over mindless chit chat.  Nothing important is shared between the two.  Smiles and laughter fill the kitchen.  Neither have had a breakfast together without the hustle and bustle of getting kids ready, themselves ready and heading out the door on time.  The enjoyment is felt between the two of them as they start their day as easily and mindfully as a couple with children could possibly dream.

"Well, I'm officially stuffed," Chris leans back and pats his belly.  "That was delicious, Scarlet.  Thank you so much for that wonderful surprise."

"Umm, before you go; could I talk to you?"  Scarlet places the paper plates in the trash since the creep who broke in destroyed all their china.  "You know that I'm scared because of all the weird things going on around here, right?"

"Yes, I'm aware of that," Chris nods his head.

"Well, I was wondering if we could get a dog.  I think that having a dog would make me feel more at ease around here."

Chris ponders her question for a moment before responding.  "I think that's a fantastic idea, honey.  Having a dog or two on the farm wouldn't be a bad idea at all."

"Really?  I was hoping you'd agree.  I think it's a great compromise.  I quit nagging you to leave but feel a little safer here at the same time," a smile spreads across her face.

"Well, it's settled then. We will go and get a new puppy this evening. If you have a chance, pick up a newspaper while you're in town and we can look through it and see what is being offered in the classifieds." He kisses her cheek and heads out to the fields for the day.

Scarlet got the kids off to school with ease this morning. It seems that rising early gives her time to wake up a bit before the hustle and bustle of getting kids ready and out the door. Things ran a lot smoother than she expected. *Maybe I'll wake early every morning,* she thinks as she pulls into a vacant parking spot in front of the local grocery store, Mel's One Stop Shop.

"Good morning, Scarlet," Nancy Sherpa greets Scarlet as she exits her vehicle. Nancy is an older woman with graying black hair. Her eyes are a piercing blue with speckles of gold. She stands just an inch or so taller than Scarlet. She is married to the town pastor, Ned Sherpa, who presided over Carl and Mary Ellen's funeral, Chris' parents.

"Hello, Nancy. It's a pleasure bumping into you," Scarlet leans in for a hug. "Would you like some help loading your groceries in the car?"

"Oh, yes dear. I would really appreciate that. It seems the older I get, the harder it is for me to do the most simple of tasks." Nancy was diagnosed with Multiple Sclerosis two years ago. Every day that passes, chores that require her motor skills become harder to complete.

"Oh, it's understandable. How have you and Ned been? I haven't seen you two in quite a while."

"Yeah, it was Carl and Mary Ellen's funeral that we last saw each other. Things are okay on our end. How are things with you? Are you guys settling in alright?"

Scarlet is a bit hesitant. She wants to scream *hell no* but instead, takes a deep breath and lies through her teeth. "Oh, we're settling in just fine. The kids enjoy the school here and Chris loves working on the old farm. Some days I wonder what drove him so far away from home. The farm life seems to suit him a lot better than the life we had back in Los Angeles."

Nancy cocks her head to the side and lowers her eyebrows. "Well, I don't know what caused him to leave but I know that he left not long after his sister had her baby."

*Sister? Baby? Chris never told me anything about having a sister.* "Um, excuse me. What do you mean after his sister had her baby? I thought that Chris was an only child; or at least that's what he said was his reason for staying here and living on the family farm."

"Oh, I'm sorry. I shouldn't have said anything but I thought you knew. I don't know what happened to her son, but she passed away about six months after Chris left, so he technically is the only child; or at least the only child left." Nancy's face is somber, sadness spreading from one end of it to the other.

"Oh, I don't know why he never brought her up but maybe her memory is just too much for him," Scarlet makes excuses, her anger dissipating instantly. *Poor Chris; he's been through so much and I didn't even know the half of it. Now I feel like a total ass trying to make him sell his family farm. Stupid!*

"Well, it was nice running into you and thank you so much for helping me load my groceries. I really appreciate it," Nancy wraps Scarlet in a tender hug.

"Oh, anytime; anytime at all. You take care Nancy and I hope to run into you soon."

Scarlet makes her way into Mel's One Stop Shop. She needs to replace all the items that were broken last night. *First things, first; we need dishes.* Scarlet makes her way to aisle one where all the kitchen items were. She grabs two sets of the plain white dishes before making her way over to the aisle with the telephones.

# Avance

*Now, I could have sworn there was a phone jack upstairs so I'll buy two phones just in case,* she thinks to herself as she reaches up and grabs two corded phones and places them in her cart.

The last items on her list were picture frames. *Damn, I wish there was a Dollar Store around here. Five dollars for a small picture frame is absurd.* She turns the cart around without putting one single picture frame in her cart.

"Hi, Mrs. Haggis," a young cashier says. Her name tag reads Charlotte.

"Um, hi Charlotte," Scarlet responds politely, not knowing who this girl is. "How are you?"

A chuckle breaks from the young girl. "You don't remember me do you?"

"No, I don't. Should I?" Scarlet asks, confusion spreading across her face.

"No, not really. I attended your in-laws funeral. I'm Charlotte Glesson. My mom is the event coordinator at the church. She's the one that helped you plan the funeral."

*Oh shit! That's right. I met her a couple of times.* "Oh, I'm sorry. That was a difficult time for my family and it all seems like such a blur. Now I remember you. How are you and your parents…?" Scarlet trails off; forgetting her parents' names.

"Joe and Clarissa Gleeson; they're fine. Mom is planning a couple of events at the church and Dad is farming the field, as always," Charlotte replies as she scans the items through the register. "How is everyone in your family? The kids settling into school?"

"Oh, yeah. We're doing well. The kids seemed to settle in very quickly. I wasn't sure how they would adjust to the move but it seems to be rubbing off well on them."

"Well that's good to hear. I see Charlie at school. He seems to be an easy person to get along with and he's quite popular."

This causes Scarlet to raise her brows. "How popular?"

"Oh, not like that..." Charlotte responds, quickly realizing that Scarlet thinks he's popular with the ladies.

"Why aren't you in school?" Scarlet grabs a couple of bills from her wallet to pay for her purchases.

"I'm in a work experience class. Two hours a day, I work here in place of a class."

"Oh, that sounds great. Helps prepare you for the real world," Scarlet gives Charlotte a smile before accepting the change for her purchase.

# Avance

"Yes.  That's what my momma says," Charlotte smiles.  "Have a great day, Mrs. Haggis," Charlotte says as Scarlet pushes her cart out.

*What a nice young lady.  Her and Charlie would look so cute together.*  Scarlet thinks about her son dating and then stops herself before the daydreaming starts. *No way!  He's too young to date.  Nope, not anytime* soon!

Scarlet loads her two bags into the back of the car and pushes the cart back to the entrance of the store.  She rounds the car to the drivers' side door.  A gasp escapes her mouth at the sight before her.

# CHAPTER SEVEN

Scarlet doesn't know whether to be livid or terrified.  Both of the driver side tires have been slashed.  She runs her hands through her long hair and lets out a heavy sigh.  *This shit is getting ridiculous!*

Scarlet growls as she walks toward the store.  *Just another fucked up thing and no way was this an accident.  Someone deliberately slashed those tires!!!*

"Hi, Charlotte, may I use the phone?  I'm having car problems."  *Yeah, car problems, my ass!*

"Sure, Mrs. Haggis.  The phone is over there," Charlotte points towards the manager's office.  "Don't worry, he allows people to use the phone all the time," she smiles at her and continues to ring customers up.

Scarlet walks to the manager's office and dials the operator for a tow truck. *This is going to cost us an arm and a leg, I'm sure.* "Yes, I need a tow at Mel's One Stop Shop," she tells the woman on the other end.

"Yes ma'am, can you tell me what's going on?" The lady on the other end of the line asks.

"Um, well it seems the tires of my car have been slashed and I will need a tow to the nearest auto shop."

"I'm so sorry, ma'am. I will get a tow truck to you in the next twenty minutes."

After the details are given to Scarlet about the wait time, she sighs as she places the receiver back on its cradle and walks back out to her car to wait. "Thanks, Charlotte," Scarlet says as she passes her register.

"Any time Mrs. Haggis," she shoots her a gorgeous smile.

Chris hasn't had any issues in the fields today. The tractor hasn't broken down once and the seedlings are beginning to sprout. *This is the*

*life,* he thinks to himself before heading back the house for lunch.

Sitting at the nook eating his turkey sandwich, his mind travels back to another time. A time when he and Laura were one and the world was right. Maybe not really right since no one could know of their love, but at least it felt right between them.

Laura's hair shined in the moonlight. Her green eyes danced with wonder and curiosity. She was absolutely the most beautiful woman on the earth.

"Chris," she looks up at him. "Why won't anyone accept our love? Why do we have to sneak around and keep it hidden?" A somber look filling her face.

"I don't know, Laura. I guess they just don't want to accept things they don't understand. Simple minded folks live in simple little towns and they seem to have to have their say in everyone else's lives," was the only response that he could think of.

"Well, how are we supposed to keep our love alive when we have to sneak around to see each other? To me, it doesn't seem worth being with someone if we can't be open about it."

Chris let out a deep sigh. "Honey, we have to keep this a secret, at least in this town. Once you turn eighteen, we will pack up our things and we will move far away from here. Away from the prying eyes of a small town and away from the place where everyone knows us and everyone knows our business," he whispered in her ear as he wrapped his arms around her tiny waist. The barn was their spot. Theirs and no one else's.

"Could we move to a big city like Chicago or Los Angeles or New York City?' Her eyes danced with wonder and voice shrieked in pitch.

A chuckle escaped him. "We can go anywhere your heart desires," he kissed her lips and held her close.

Scarlet arrived home just in time for dinner. Since she ran into issues with the car she decided to just grab a couple of pizzas at Tony's Pizzeria.

"Mommy got pizza," James hollers from the front yard when Scarlet exits the car holding two square boxes.

"It's pizza night!" Audrey and Suzanne scream in tandem. Those girls love pizza.

"Yes guys, Momma picked up pizza. You can't start a Friday night without pizza and a movie," she says as she pulls a Disney DVD from her purse. "Get in the house and wash up so we can eat and watch our movie," she ushers the kids into the house.

Without a fight, the three young Haggis children race to the bathroom and wash up. Scarlet places the pizza boxes on the counter in the kitchen and pulls out the paper plates from the cabinet. Each plate gets a slice of pizza except for Chris and Charlie's plate which holds two slices.

"Hey, Mom," Charlie's voice directs Scarlet to the fridge. "Oh cool, pizza for dinner," he says as he pulls out a bottle of water.

"Yeah, I spent far too long in town today and didn't want to cook so pizza it is," she explained as Chris walked into the room.

"Well, I can't imagine ending this week without pizza and....*Frozen*," he rolls his eyes as he picks up the movie on the counter; disappointment filling his face.

Scarlet giggles, "Don't worry, Charlie. I got an action packed movie for us for after the younger kids go to bed."

"Thank God!" A smile replaces the disappointment. Charlie would never ever admit it but he has cried at the end of a few of the Disney movies. He may act tough but he has a tender heart.

# Avance

"Why don't you go get washed up and help the younger kids clean up too? I'll pour the drinks and see you guys in the family room," Scarlet smiles as she finishes up in the kitchen.

He takes a drag off his cigarette and exhales slowly. Anger and frustration are quickly creeping into every crevice of his being. *They aren't taking my messages seriously. I'm going to have to up my game and soon.*

He field strips his smoke and shoves his hands into his pockets. His mind is racing a million miles a minute. How can he terrorize them more? Is it time to get serious and show them who's boss? All these thoughts cross his mind as he pulls another smoke from his left shirt pocket and places it between his lips. A strike from his Zippo and a deep inhale of the sweet tobacco begins to calm his nerves.

He creeps, ever so quietly, to the front window of the farm house—the farm house that he should be living in. He notices the family sitting around the television, eating their pizza and watching a movie. *What a precious scene,* he thinks sarcastically.

He turns his back and heads to the driveway where the old truck and family car sits. *It would be a shame if something were to happen to their cars.* He reaches his hand in his pocket and bends down by the front, drivers' side tire. A swift slice of his blade and his goal has been achieved; now, to wait and watch his plan unfold.

# CHAPTER EIGHT

The Haggis family stayed up well past their normal bed times—Chris especially so. His mind was racing with memories and fantasies that were once behind him. A ghost of memories past haunted his every moment. Laura was his whole world and then she wasn't. He moved on—she moved on, but did he ever really move on? Or did he just simply try to push her memories from his conscious and place them in the depths of his brain?

No matter what really happened, the truth is she's back—haunting every part of him. He can't even look at Scarlet the same as he once did. No, he thought he loved her—truly loved her, but that's not the case. The move back to Nebraska has proven that ten-fold. He loves and longs for Laura but he can never have her. Not again. Not after she did what she did.

"Come back to earth there gorgeous," Scarlet's voice pulls him back to the kitchen in the farm house and his cup of hot Joe. "Wow, you were like a million miles away. Are you alright?"

"Yeah, I'm fine. I just didn't sleep well last night," he half lies. "What are you doing up so early?"

"Oh, I wanted to look through the classifieds of the newspaper and see if there were any puppies or young dogs available within a hundred mile radius of us."

He puts his coffee mug on the nook, " that's right, we were looking for puppies today."

"Puppies!" A little voice shrieks behind them. Audrey, their little early bird, has quietly crept down the old staircase without making a sound. "Are we getting a puppy?" she squeals, pure excitement coursing through her body.

"Quiet now, we are going to look and see what's available," Scarlet rises from her seat to make Audrey her morning cereal.

# Avance

After all the Haggis family members were up and ready, the whole clan headed out to the family car to look at potential puppies. Scarlet found three litters within twenty-five miles of the family home. All of the children were excited about bringing home a new puppy. Scarlet, for the first time in a long time, smiled a genuine smile as she looked at her family. Hope for the future was great now.

"Ok, we aren't guaranteeing that we are getting a puppy today. We are just looking at the puppies. We may not find any that appeal to us," Scarlet tries to make it very clear to her three young children. Charlie doesn't have to be reminded of this.

"I want a girl puppy and name her Sparkly," Suzanne chimes in, ignoring everything her mother just said.

"No, I want to name her Glitter," Audrey pipes in.

"No way. We're getting a boy dog and I'm naming him Poop Eater!" James asserted himself.

Both girls begin to shriek and cry at the name that James picked out for their puppy. "Now, James, no one is naming our puppy Poop Eater. How in the world did you even come up with that name?" Scarlet questions.

"Well, dogs eat poop so the only logical name should be Poop Eater," he says grinning from ear to ear.

"Well, we aren't naming any dog that—end of story!" Scarlet closes the car door.

Chris lets out a laugh as he puts the car in drive and heads out of the circled driveway.

He stands, out of view, in the orchard across from the old farmhouse. The almond trees hide his location but he can see the Haggis family loading up in their car for their Saturday outing. The little ones are fighting about names of some sort while the mother is fighting to quiet them down.

"No, the dad and oldest son aren't supposed to be in the car," he mutters under his breath when he sees Chris and Charlie get inside. "This is not supposed to happen this way," he growls, frustration seeping through every word like a knife through butter.

There isn't anything he can do now. What's done is done and all he can do is look on with horror as the car speeds off down the street. *What have I done?*

# Avance

The kids are singing, off key, to a Warrant song. The girls love cherry pie and the song is no different. Charlie is trying to get them to sing quietly but there is no stopping these little divas. They are singing their hearts out without a care in the world.

"Chris, you need to slow down," Scarlet warns, pointing out that the stop sign is growing closer.

"I'm trying," Chris responds in a calm and quiet voice. "The brake pedal is all the way to the floor but we aren't slowing down."

Scarlet's heart is racing and sweat is forming along Chris' brow. This stop sign stops traffic in their direction but not in the other directions.

"Dad, stop—there's a big rig coming," Charlie yells, not knowing there isn't a damn thing his father can do. "Please stop!"

Before Chris could say a word, they cross through the intersection and almost make it through before the big rig plows into their back quarter panel. The car is spinning out of control. They have no clue which way they are facing when a farm truck hit them coming from the other direction.

The car is smoking, glass lies all around them. There's no movement from any of the family members inside. Blood is dripping as the drivers of the two trucks circle around yelling things at each other and making calls for emergency personnel. Chris is trying to stay conscious but the darkness is engulfing him. He struggles to breathe, to make sure his family is alive. The world becomes darker until the darkness consumes him.

# CHAPTER NINE

Laura pushed her final push and welcomed a second baby boy into the world. A little boy with pink skin and a cry that could wake the dead was brought into this world. Chris' mother and father were there to witness the birth but not with faces of joy. Oh no, his parents were beyond livid at the sight that had unfolded before them in the family barn—the barn that Chris had professed his love to Laura in.

"How the fuck could you do this to our family, boy?" His father, Carl, yelled at him. "This is a fucking abomination! Not only one abomination but two? How the fuck could you?" Carl's blue eyes glared at Chris. Anger was an understatement for what his father felt at that moment. Chris fucked up and he knew damn well how bad he'd fucked up.

"I-I'm sorry dad. I don't know what happened. I guess I just let my heart override my brain," were the only words that he could find.

"Love? LOVE!! This isn't love, Chris. Jesus Christ! This is...I don't even know the word for what this is but goddammit boy, this is the biggest fuck up you've ever had," his father shouted as Laura shook and cried in the barn. Chris' mother, Mary Ellen, was tending to the babies and didn't give two shits about the woman who'd just given birth to them.

"Dad, I need to get to Laura," Chris said. His heart pounded and his body wanted to be near the woman he loved more than it wanted its next breath of air.

"The hell you're going anywhere near her! You're going to pack your shit up and you're going to get the fuck out of town. I don't want to see your face or hear your voice ever again," his father said, eyes narrowed and lips pursed.

"You can't do that. Those are my children in there!"

"Oh, you care about those abominations? Fine, you can take one. Hell you can take them both.

In fact, I wish you would.  Take them and get the fuck out of here you sorry excuse of a man!"

His father's words cut like a knife.  One can't help who they fall in love with.  It just sort of happens.  Why didn't anyone understand that? What could he do to stay with Laura and live a spectacular life with her?

Steady and rhythmic beeping draws Chris out of the darkness.  Beeping of machines and jumbling of voices is all he can hear.  His head aches and his body is screaming in pain.

"Chris…Chris, can you hear me?  Do you know where you are?" A strange man's voice is calling out to him but it hurts too bad to move—too bad to move even his mouth.

"Chris, you're in the hospital.  You've been in a terrible accident," the man's voice continues on. "I'm Doctor Stephenson.  I'm going to take good care of you."

Doctor George Stephenson is an older gentleman with white hair and wire framed glasses.  He's been employed with Mercy General Hospital for nearly twenty years.  He knew the Haggis family when their children were just tiny tots.  In fact, he had set and treated Chris' arm the summer he fell out of the barn and broke it in two.

"Family," is all Chris is able to spit out to the doctor and nurses around him.

"Your family is being treated here. All of you survived," is the only information that Chris was able to receive but it was all that he needed before the darkness consumed him once again.

He stalks the hospital rooms, bouncing from one room to another. It's surprising that no one notices him stalking around, but all the employees are busy trying to save the lives of all the Haggis family members. Suzanne was the most severely injured and they are rushing her in for emergency surgery. *All the surgery in the world won't save her—not if her mom doesn't take her and her other siblings and run. Run as far away from Greenwich as possible.*

The mysterious being creeps out of the hospital undetected. He makes his way through the parking lot to the very last row. He climbs into the stolen car and heads toward the Haggis farm. One day, one day soon, that farm will be his. It will finally be in the hands of the rightful heir.

Scarlet lies in her bed, head wrapped in bandages and her face is bloody and bruised. Her ribs ache as the pain killers slowly wear off.

# Avance

*Every part of my body is on fire. What the hell happened? Where is my family?*

"Hi, Mrs. Haggis. How are you feeling today?" a nurse asks as she fumbles with the IV machine.

"I-I...what happened?" Scarlet is confused and unable to process anything. She has no clue as to what happened or where her family is.

"You were in an accident. You were banged up really bad," the nurse explains, without making eye contact with her.

"My...my family? What happened to them," she sobs, hoping that she tells her that they are all safe and sound and she was the only one injured.

"Hey now, don't go getting your heart rate up on me. They all survived and are all in other rooms," she places a tender hand on Scarlet's shoulder.

The nurse pushes some medicine through Scarlet's IV and she becomes tired. Her eyes are heavy and her head is foggy but she still has questions. *How is Audrey? Is Suzanne okay? What about James? Where is Chris? Is Charlie doing alright? No, I don't want the darkness to take me before I get my answers.*

The darkness claims Scarlet. No dreams or nightmares exist, just darkness. Her thoughts are quieted in a medical induced euphoria. No pain, no cares and no thoughts. Nothing but peace washes over Scarlet.

# CHAPTER TEN

*It's been three weeks since the Haggis family's accident. Chris has healed from most of his injuries and has been released to go home. "I want to go see my kids," he tells the nurse as he signs his discharge papers and hands them back to her.*

*"Well, now that you are medically discharged, you can go anywhere you'd like. I'll take you to the pediatric ward and show you their rooms but first, your wife wants to see you," the nurse explains. In the three weeks Chris has been in the hospital, he's never seen this nurse before but then again, he could've and just forgotten.*

*His short term memory was damaged from hitting the side window in the accident.*

*"Thank you, Nurse….." he trails off.*

*"Call me Sandra. We've met once before but that was about eight days ago," she reminds him gently.*

*"Oh yeah, that's right," he lies. "I've had so many nurses over the past three weeks that they all start to look the same."*

*"Yeah, I guess we all look alike," she chuckles as she makes sure all the IVs are removed. "Well, my friend, you're free to go."*

*Chris makes his way down the hall to Scarlet's room. All her IVs have been removed but her head is still wrapped up and her face is discolored. "Baby?" Chris says as he quietly enters her bedroom.*

*"Chris, honey they released you," she says in a near whisper. "Are the kids released yet?"*

*He pulls a chair up next to her bed. "I don't think so. The nurse said she would take me to the pediatric floor to see them soon," he takes her hand in his and strokes the top of it with his thumb.*

*"That's good. The kids need one of us with them."*

*"Yeah, they sure do. Especially Suzanne—you know how terrified of the dark she is."*

*"Yeah, that little girl sure does fear things that aren't even there."*

*"I wonder where she gets that from," Chris eyes Scarlet with a smirk.*

*"Chris, how did all of this happen?" Scarlet tries to hold in her tears.*

*He hangs his head in defeat. "I don't know. There isn't a logical reason that any of this was an accident," Chris says, quietly—almost to himself.*

*Heavy steps and a knock at the door cause the two to whip their heads around. "Mr. and Mrs. Haggis?" a tall man in a Sheriff's uniform questions with his hat in his hand.*

*"Yes?" Chris says.*

*"I'm Deputy Faulkner—Alexander Faulkner. I'm the deputy investigating your accident. May I come in?"*

*"Please," Chris rises from his chair with a groan.*

*"No, no, please stay seated," the deputy says as he grabs a chair from out in the hall and brings it in. "I have a few questions," He takes a seat and clears his throat.*

*Scarlet and Chris adjust themselves and give the deputy their full attention. "What can we help you with?" Chris asks holding his wife's hand.*

*"Well, the Sheriff's department has completed our investigation. It was determined that your accident really was more intentional. The brake line was cut clean through."*

*"What?" Scarlet gasps. "Chris, whoever was terrorizing us is now trying to kill us," she begins to cry.*

*"You're jumping to conclusions baby," Chris tries to comfort her.*

*"Terrorizing you? We have no reports of any terrorism," Deputy Faulkner responds looking confused.*

*"No, we didn't report it. We received a phone call not too long after we moved here and then someone broke in and ransacked the house two nights before the accident," Chris explains.*

*"Can you tell me where your son, Charlie, was during those events?" Deputy Faulkner looks between Chris and Scarlet.*

*"Charlie? Why would you want to know where Charlie was?" Scarlet becomes irritated at the line of questioning.*

*"Ma'am, I just need to know for my report. We had something come up in the investigation and I need to follow up on it."*

*"Well with the phone call, Charlie was with me," Chris answers.*

*"And when the house was ransacked, he was out at dinner with the entire family," Scarlet defends her son.*

*"I only ask because the crime lab found some blood on the brake line and a partial fingerprint. The blood tested back to Charlie but the fingerprint is still unknown," Alexander explained.*

*"There has to be a mistake. Charlie was in the car with us. If he cut the line, wouldn't he have made sure to not be in the car when we left?" Scarlet reasons, more for her own sanity than for anything else.*

*"Does Charlie have any close friends?" Alexander continues, avoiding Scarlet's question entirely.*

*"No. We just moved here and he hasn't had an opportunity to make any friends," Chris is becoming worried for his eldest son and his family.*

*Alexander continues to make notes on his note pad. What seemed like an open and shut case has now become an absolute mystery. How did the blood of Charlie Haggis get on the brake line if he didn't cut it himself? Does he have friends that his parents don't know about? Why would he get into a car that he knew couldn't stop? Knowing he can't answer the questions right now, he rises to his feet.*

*"Thank you for your time Mr. Haggis, Mrs. Haggis." Alexander bows his head. "I will need to talk to Charlie in the near future but I will wait until he has been discharged and both of you can be present for the questioning." Alexander forces a smile at the couple.*

*"Thank you, Deputy. I appreciate you waiting until he is discharged and we are there before you question him," Chris says as he rises and begins to walk with him out of the room.*

*"Well, it's protocol that all minors have an adult present when answering any questions. I'll be in touch." Alexander turns and walks down the hallway.*

# CHAPTER ELEVEN

The entire Haggis family was reunited five weeks after the horrific car accident. Scarlet was released just two days after Chris. Charlie and Audrey came home three days later while James came home two days after that. Suzanne, the one with the most significant injuries, came home seven days after James. While all their injuries varied, Suzanne's was the most life threatening. A fractured vertebra, ruptured spleen, broken ribs, a punctured lung and two broken legs left her in the Pediatric Intensive Care for three weeks before being moved onto the pediatric ward for the last two weeks.

"Thank goodness we are all home," Chris says after he and Scarlet finally get all the kids in bed. He honestly wasn't sure if they could've survived much longer. With Suzanne in the hospital, Scarlet never wanted to leave the hospital but she had to in order to rest and heal herself. Chris was happy that everyone was finally home and he and Scarlet weren't ripping each other's heads off about her health.

The town folk tended to the farm while they were all in the hospital and they are still tending to it so Chris and Charlie can continue to heal from their ordeal. The women in town have brought dinner out to them every night since Chris came home and plan on continuing until Scarlet is healed enough to take care of that herself.

"Amen to that, and thank goodness for such an amazing group of people from town looking after us," Scarlet says.

"You wouldn't find that in Los Angeles," Chris responds, taking a drink of his warm tea.

"No, but we probably wouldn't have been in such a horrible accident either," Scarlet snickers, being truthful and honest with Chris.

"Why is it that you think every time something less than stellar happens that it's because of this damn town? Bad things happen all the damn time, Scarlet. It doesn't mean that someone is trying to kill us. Geez," Chris remarks as he rises from his seat and heads to the kitchen. "You just need to knock this shit off," he says before exiting the room.

"No," Scarlet yells to him as he ascends the stairs. "I won't knock this shit off. You're fucking pigheaded and stubborn and you're going to get us all fucking killed because of your damn pride." She heaves oxygen into her lungs. She said all of that, angrily, without taking a single breath.

Scarlet sits there, dumbfounded at the conversation that just took place. She's not normally an angry person and she hates being angry, especially at Chris, but damn, he's pushing all her buttons. *Why doesn't he see what I see? The brake line was intentionally cut and even the deputy verified that but because suspicion lies on Charlie, he doesn't want to believe it. No, Charlie didn't do it but someone did and he just refuses to acknowledge it.*

After a few moments, Scarlet decides to head to bed. Her body is still sore and now her head aches from dealing with Chris. *A good sleep in a comfy bed will make everything alright again.* She slowly makes her way up the staircase and into her room.

Chris stands in the kitchen for a long period. The light behind him gives the stalker visual.

# Twisted Destiny

*What is he thinking about? Why won't his family just get the message and go back home?*

He takes a long drag off his smoke and exhales slowly. The nicotine calms his nerves with each long, drawn out drag he takes. Since stalking the Haggis family, his habit has taken on a world of its own. Instead of half a pack a day, he is almost up to two packs a day. *Something has to give and soon or I'm going to go broke buying these things,* he thinks as he strips the smoke and places the filter in his pocket. *No evidence for DNA.*

Chris stands, staring off into the distance. Scarlet really gets his blood boiling when she refuses to let something go. *Ugh, she gets something in her head and then she doesn't know when to shut up about it.* Laura...Laura was the best thing he ever had and this move is proving it to him. They were in love. Never argued or disagreed. No, they were perfect for each other. They would still be together if it weren't for his parents. Chris' parents are what drove a wedge between them; the only reason Chris grabbed Charlie and left Nebraska all together.

*At least I have her memories,* he thinks as his thoughts drift back to the last time he saw Laura before leaving for Los Angeles.

# Avance

The December wind whipped around them as her contractions began. Her parents had been pressuring her to reveal the name of the father but she refused. Tonight, the name would have to be revealed for Chris refused to leave her side. "Baby, take deep breaths," he said as he held her close to his body as they made their way to the barn—the barn where all of this started and where all of this would end.

"Chris, it hurts," she whined as another contraction took hold of her. Her abdominal muscles squeezing tightly as her hand gripped Chris' just as tight.

"I know it hurts," he lied. No way could he have known the pain she was enduring nor would he ever know that kind of pain.

He gets her into the barn and situated on a hay stack. "I love you, Laura. With all my heart and soul I love you and nothing will ever change that," he said, bending down. He pressed his lips to hers as another contraction began.

"What the fuck is going on in here?" an angry voice bellowed behind them.

Chris rises, quickly, and staggers backward. "Nothing Dad, umm, Laura went into labor and well...I was helping her get situated. I was going to come fetch you and Mom..."

"Don't fucking lie to me boy," Carl growled at his son. "I don't fucking like liars!"

Not knowing what to say, Chris just stood there, staring back at his father. Unable to make eye contact, he stared over his father's head and found a spider web to keep his gaze fixed on.

"Dammit Chris, get the fuck out of here. I'm so disgusted in you that I can't even look at you at the moment. She…you…this pregnancy is against God! It's against nature. Ugh, you two make me sick," Carl took his eyes away from Chris and fixed them on Laura. "You two sicken me!"

Chris snaps himself back into the present. That memory is the hardest memory to think about. The day that his and Laura's love was exposed and the world judged them. Anger and shame begin to rise at the same time within Chris' soul. How could one feel both anger and shame at the same time? No one is for certain but one thing is for sure—Chris was feeling both.

"Honey, are you coming to bed?" Scarlet's voice is a whisper behind him.

"Huh, what time is it?" Chris turns to face her.

"It's after one in the morning."

"Damn, it's that late? I didn't realize I had been standing here for that long." Chris shakes his head, unable to believe it's that late and he hasn't even been to sleep yet.

"That must have been some thought you were thinking about," Scarlet says, curiously.

"Yeah, it was but it's in the past and that's where it needs to remain," he responds, trying to convince himself more than Scarlet. "I'm sorry for snapping at you earlier. I know this place has you on edge but..." Scarlet stops him before he can finish.

"It's okay. Let's just forget it for now. I'm too tired to talk about it."

"Ok. Come on, let's go to bed," Chris places his hand on the small of Scarlet's back and leads her toward the stairs.

# CHAPTER TWELVE

The past two weeks since being released from the hospital have been quiet. The children rest most of the time, either sleeping or watching television, and Scarlet and Chris lounge around, glad for the help from the town's people.

It was mid-morning on a Monday when a tap came on the front door. Chris rises and shuffles his way to answer it. He looks out the window and see's Deputy Faulkner on the other side of the door. *Fuck! What does he want? To accuse my son of something else now?*

# Avance

With hesitation, Chris unlocks the deadbolt and opens the door. "Good morning, Deputy," Chris says, trying to keep the disdain out of his voice.

"Good morning, Mr. Haggis. You can call me Alexander, if you'd like," Alexander begins the interview. "I have a few questions I need to ask. Is now a good time?"

"Are you planning on accusing my son of something he didn't do?" Chris gives Alexander a stern look.

"No, Mr. Haggis. That is not my intention. I just need to figure out how his blood got there and if he may know whose partial print was on the brake line. I'm just doing my job."

Chris opens the door wider and steps back to allow the deputy entry into his home. As the deputy crosses the threshold, he removes his hat. "I'll make this as quick as possible but I will need to talk to Charlie as well," Alexander is blunt and to the point.

"Well, doesn't he have the right to an attorney?" Chris questions, trying to defend his son—the son that he and Laura created together. The only perfect child that came from her.

"Mr. Haggis, he only needs an attorney if he's hiding something or if I place him under arrest. Right now, all I need is a parent to be in the room with him as I ask him some questions."

Chris eyes the deputy, unsure whether he trusts him or not. "Please, have a seat and I'll get my wife and son," Chris shows Deputy Faulkner to the dining room table. "Would you like something to drink?" He asks, trying to be polite and show some manners.

"I'm fine, but thank you," Alexander says as he grabs a note pad and pen from his left breast pocket.

Chris fetches both Scarlet and Charlie. "You two," he says when he finds them sitting on the back porch, enjoying the mid-morning sun. "Deputy Faulkner is here and would like to speak to all of us."

"What for?" Charlie questions, not knowing what he could have done or knows to warrant a visit by law enforcement.

"I don't know but if you get off your butt and get inside, we'll know soon enough," Chris slightly fibs to his oldest son. He doesn't want to open up that can of worms out here. Charlie needs to cooperate with the deputy so they can put all of this behind them.

The three members of the family circle around the table and stare at the deputy at the end. "Thank you for giving up some of your time to answer some questions," Deputy Faulkner starts off. "I just have a couple of questions for Charlie," he continues.

# Avance

"Why me?" Charlie's stomach begins to form knots and a lump develops in his throat.

"Well son, I just have some questions that I believe only you can answer." Alexander gives Charlie a slight smile trying to put the teenager at ease.

Charlie nods his head; words are unable to form because of the butterflies residing in the pit of his stomach. He has no clue what this interview could be about and he's scared, but he would never admit it. He doesn't know anything more than his parents. Any questions that the deputy has would be in vain.

"Ok, so let's get this started," Alexander forces a smile. "Charlie, where were you the day before the accident?"

"What? Why does that matter?" Charlie questions, not fully understanding what the scope of this interview is.

"Just answer the questions, son," Alexander presses. He was a bit more harsh than he had anticipated.

"I was at school and then I came home and worked with my dad." Sweat begins to form on Charlie's face. A red hue spreads across his cheeks as he diverts his eyes to his fingers.

"So, you weren't anywhere near the car that day?" Alexander continues, knowing that the boy either has something to hide or is truly nervous. He would bet that the boy is hiding something and, if he had his way, he would get to the bottom of it—like right now.

"No. Why would I have been?" Charlie is genuinely confused. His eyes dart up and meet Alexander and hold his gaze. Someone lying or being deceptive would not be able to maintain eye contact for that long.

"I don't know, that's why I'm asking you." Alexander is sure he doesn't have the right suspect but that wouldn't account for the DNA that was discovered.

Charlie just sits there, stone cold. There was no reason for him to be near the car that day.

"Charlie, is there any reason…any at all, that your DNA would be on the brake line of that car?"

Confusion and fear wash over Charlie's face. He has no idea where this line of questioning is going, but he sure doesn't like it. "No. I've never touched the brake line of the car nor have I ever worked on the car. My DNA should only be inside the car," he responds, disdain and anger sweeping over him. No one likes to be accused of something they didn't do, and Charlie is no exception.

"Son, then can you explain why we found your DNA—blood, on the brake line and a partial, unidentified fingerprint?" Alexander's tone is becoming more accusing and less friendly.

Charlie is taken aback at the question. He has no clue how his blood got there or whose partial print that was but he was certain of one thing. "That's not my blood or a fingerprint from anyone I know. I think your lab made a mistake. Now, if you have no more questions, I'm leaving."

"Son, I'm not done asking questions. You need to sit back down," Deputy Faulkner says as Charlie gets up.

"I think my son said he was done answering questions, Deputy," Scarlet jumps in. "If you have any further questions for my son, you can contact our attorney." She turns to Charlie and lightly touches his hand. "Go ahead and go to your room Charlie."

"Now, there's no reason to get defensive if you have nothing to hide," Alexander says. "Only guilty people need attorneys."

"And the innocent when an overzealous deputy starts barking up the wrong tree," Scarlet snarls at him—mama bear mode taking full effect. "Now, as I said, if you have any other questions, you can contact our attorney. Chris, show this *wonderful* deputy the door," she says sarcastically.

Chris escorts the deputy to the door. "Deputy, you are barking up the wrong tree. I don't know how my son's blood ended up on that brake line, but I can assure you, he harbors no ill will to us and we love him and we all have respect for each other. I think you need to stop focusing on him and start focusing on other avenues," Chris bids the deputy a farewell.

"Dad," Charlie startles Chris. "What is going on? Why would my DNA be on the brake line of the car?" Charlie looks nervous and scared, and rightfully so.

"Son," Chris wraps his arm around Charlie's shoulders. "I don't know, but I'm sure we will get it all figured out." Chris lies to his child. He's pretty sure he knows what's going on and who is doing this but he can't tell Charlie without exposing the secret he's held for fifteen years.

# CHAPTER THIRTEEN

Four weeks after their release from the hospital, the Haggis family is finally on their own. No more town women bringing dinners or cleaning the house or doing laundry and no more town men to plow the fields or fixing broke tractors. Everyone is fully functional and pulling their own weight around the place.

Deputy Faulkner hasn't been back to the property since he interrogated Charlie. However, Scarlet called her old law firm and received a referral to a criminal defense attorney in Omaha. Jeremy O'Riley was a well-known and established attorney and had attended law school with Scarlet's prior employer. He decided to take the case pro-bono but was sure his services weren't needed because there wasn't any evidence that could lead to a conviction.

"Honey, I think we really should just pack up and go back to Los Angeles," Scarlet says, as she and Chris crawl into bed. "This move here has been one hell of a ride and nothing positive has come from it." Fear over this conversation consumes her but she has to express her feelings to her husband. She doesn't feel safe in this town and he has a right to know.

Chris sighs, "I know babe. I know. It's just…I have some good memories in this house that I thought I had lost after I moved. When I left, it was under bad circumstances and coming back has stirred up memories I'd forgotten about."

"What type of memories?"

Chris' heart begins to race. He doesn't want to divulge those memories to Scarlet. They're his special memories and she wouldn't understand. "Oh, just memories of the good times with my parents. The blow up after Charlie was born was bad and it overrode the good memories."

"What about your sister? Do you have memories of your sister here too?" Scarlet questions, remembering what Nancy had said the day before the accident.

# Avance

"What? My sister? Who told you about my sister?" Chris questions as his stomach turns in knots.

"Mrs. Sherpa did. She said you left not long after your sister had her baby and she didn't know why."

*Thank God for small miracles.* "Yes, I left not long after my sister had her baby. I had Charlie to take care of and my parents were already struggling financially. Dad and I had a heated conversation the night before I left...and no, I don't want to talk about that, so I left right after she had her baby. It was for the best—it really was," Chris both explains and lies to Scarlet. There was more to the story but he didn't wish to share any of it with her.

"So you and—what was your sisters name, both had babies around the same time?"

"Marie," the lie just falls from Chris' mouth. "Her name was Marie and yes, we had babies about the same time." He wants to quit playing twenty questions. He has a past he doesn't want anyone to know about and if she keeps asking questions, she will eventually put two and two together.

"What happened to Marie's baby?"

"I-I don't know. Last I figured, my parents placed him in foster care shortly after Marie's passing and I assume he was adopted." Chris honestly didn't know what happened to his sisters' baby and, at that time, he had too much going on in his life to really give it a second thought about what happened to his nephew after his sister passed away. "How about a bedtime snack? Does that sound good to you?" He changes the subject, no longer wishing to talk about the past—or more accurately, lie about the past.

"It's too late for a snack. Why don't we just go to sleep," Scarlet knows that the only reason Chris wants a snack is to end the conversation.

"Thanks babe," he kisses her cheek and rolls over but is wide awake.

*They won't fucking leave. Why the hell won't they leave?* He questions as he stares at the farm house, the last light extinguishing for the night. His anger is beginning to consume him. For as long as he could remember, anger has been the one emotion that he could feel with the most ease.

When you're thrown away by family that is supposed to love you, anger is about the only emotion that is ever fully developed. Love and affection are taught emotions and, unfortunately for him, he was never taught to love or feel affection for another human being.

## Avance

*Well, I guess I'm going to have to play hard ball with them. If they won't leave, I'll have to make sure they have no choice but to leave or die!!!*

 A plan is forming in the depths of his brain as he crushes his smoke out on the bottom of his shoe, pockets the filter and moves along the orchard back to his shack.

# CHAPTER FOURTEEN

"Audrey, Suzanne—sit down and eat your breakfast. James, put that down and get in here," Scarlet tells the kids as she runs around the kitchen trying to get them ready for school. The power went out last night and the alarm didn't go off this morning. If she can't get these kids fed and out the door in the next fifteen minutes, they will miss the bus and she will have to drive the twenty minutes into town to drop them off. "Come on you three. Sit down and eat!" she yells, which is not like her.

"Ok, Mommy. You don't have to yell!" Suzanne sits down to finish her breakfast.

# Avance

"Yeah, Mommy; yelling isn't very nice," Audrey pipes in.

"Just sit down and eat." Scarlet's exasperated from the morning chaos. Just once, she would like her day to go off without any setbacks. Since the accident her nights have been full of nightmares. The lack of sleep has every nerve on edge.

Charlie and Chris walk in just moments later. "Hey babe," Chris plants a kiss on her cheek. "Good morning."

"There's nothing good about this morning," she rolls her eyes and begins to clear the table. "Go brush your teeth double time and grab your things," she orders the kids.

"What isn't good about today? We are all awake, healthy and alive," he tries to be optimistic.

"Well, we overslept, the kids aren't listening and, if they don't hurry," she hollers at them, "they're all going to be late for the bus and then I will have to drive them and I don't feel like driving into town."

"Is it that you don't feel like driving into town or is it because you're afraid to drive?" Chris asks, trying to psychoanalyze his wife. She hasn't rode into town since that fateful day and he knows that she probably won't ever again if he doesn't push her to do it. That's why he unplugged the alarm and then plugged it back in. The power didn't go out but she doesn't need to know that.

"You know what, you don't know everything, Chris!" She spats. "And why should I talk to you about how I feel when what I feel is never taken into consideration. I've been telling you for months that I don't want to live here anymore but you don't ever listen to me. You just change the subject, ignore me or walk away. When you move me out of this God forsaken area, I'll start opening up to you more."

She puts the plates in the sink and begins to trudge up the stairs. "Oh, and if those kids miss the bus, you can drive them into town because I'm going back to bed!" Scarlet has had enough of the bullshit today. Her nerves are frazzled and Chris' enthusiasm is starting to piss her off!

Chris' plan back fired. The kids missed the bus and Scarlet refused to leave the bedroom. She had locked the door and ignored his calls through the door.

He rushed the kids to school and arrived with ten minutes to spare. He stopped at the local hardware store to pick up grease for the tractor when he noticed a sign in the window. "Puppies! 5 Queensland Heelers. Great work dogs and protective family dogs.  Asking $250 OBO."

*We were looking for puppies the day we got into the accident.  I'm sure that if I brought home a cute little Queensland puppy that needed a home and lots of love and affection, it would soften Scarlet's heart and we can finally begin to mend what is broken.*

Chris jots down the address on the sign and heads out to see the puppies.  The farm was a bit out of his way—about twenty minutes to be exact.  With Scarlet being upset with him when he left, surely she wouldn't mind him being more than an hour late, especially if he brought home the puppy she had wanted.

Chris got turned around a few times before finally arriving at his destination.  A large farmhouse with a wraparound porch sits on fifty acres of farmland.  A large oak tree with a swing accents the property.  An adult Queensland is running around the yard with five little puppies following behind her.

Chris gets out of the car and stoops down to allow the dog to smell him.  All the puppies run up, scratching his legs and arms striving to receive attention.

"Can I help you?" A deep voice calls out from the porch.

"Yeah, I'm interested in a puppy," Chris rises to his feet and brushes his hands across his pants while moving toward the porch. He extends his hand. "I'm Chris Haggis."

"Hi Chris, I'm Joe Walters."

"Nice to meet you, Joe."

"Likewise. Now, let's go see if we can't wrangle up them puppies."

Chris follows Joe into the yard as they both begin to call for the puppies. Four of the five come running. The last little puppy is too busy exploring and sniffing the air. The puppy begins to growl and chase a leaf that is blowing across the yard.

"Is that puppy a male or a female," Chris asks, pointing at the stray little dog.

"Oh, that one is a female and the most curious little dog outta the whole bunch. My wife nicknamed her Curious Georgette," he chuckles as they both watch the puppy explore its surroundings.

"I'll take that one!"

"Are you sure?"

"Yep! How much do you want for her?"

# Avance

"I'm asking two hundred and fifty since they are purebreds."

"You've got yourself a deal."

The exchange of money and puppy is made in no time and Chris is back in his car heading home. "It's okay little one. There's no need to whimper," Chris talks in puppy talk to her.

After some time, she starts to explore the car and licks the window. The drive back home with the puppy was more fun than the drive out to the farm to get her. Chris tries to keep an eye on the road and the puppy to make sure she didn't get under his feet.

"Scarlet, I'm home," Chris announces as he comes in and puts the car keys on the counter. "I brought someone to meet you." The puppy licks at Chris' face.

"Scarlet, you aren't still mad at me, are you?"

When he receives no response, his heart starts to race. *What the hell is going on?* He takes the stairs, two at a time, until he reaches the bedroom door. He turns the knob and it opens easily.

Scarlet is lying on the bed with her arms at her side. Red puddles of liquid lie beneath each arm. Her face is pale, almost paper white. Chris rushes to her side. Kneeling down he feels for a pulse on her neck. "Scarlet, baby what did you do?" he asks after he finds a faint pulse.

He picks up the phone next to the bed and discovers there is no dial tone. Quickly, he decides to rush to the phone in the kitchen. He doesn't have time to figure out why this phone isn't working. He doesn't want to leave her side but he knows he must in order to save her life. *If only I had come home sooner. Why did I have to get that puppy?*

He makes it to the phone and dials 9-1-1. It seems like forever before the dispatcher finally picks up the line.

"Kent County 9-1-1, what is your emergency?"

"Yes, my wife—she's bleeding, hurry." Chris is beginning to sweat profusely. His mind is on his wife and her alone. *I can't lose her!*

"Ok sir, I'll have someone in route quickly. What is your location?"

"81245 Township Road. Please hurry."

"I have someone in route sir. Can you tell me what happened?"

"I-I came home and found her in our bed. She's bleeding…hurry!" Chris can't think straight. His mind is all over the place. *Why would she do this to herself? I should've just moved to Los Angeles when she asked instead of demanding that we stay here. I'm so selfish.*

"Sir, we are coming as quickly as possible. Can you tell me where she is bleeding from?"

"Her wrists—she's bleeding from her wrists. She's pale and her pulse is weak." Chris' heart is beating erratically now. The fear that she may bleed to death before they get here has him on edge.

"Sir, are you with her now?"

"No. We only have a corded landline. I can't get to her."

"Sir, can you go check on her? Tell me if she's breathing and if she has a pulse."

"Yes."

"Don't hang up sir. Just place the phone on the counter and go check on her."

"Yes yes," he places the phone on the counter and races up the steps, two at a time. Sweat is dripping from his forehead as he kneels down by Scarlet. Her breathing is shallow and her pulse is faint. Blood is still pouring from the cuts on her wrists. *I have to slow down the bleeding before she bleeds to death!*

Chris rushes to the closet and finds his stash of neck ties.  He grabs two of them and rushes back to her bedside.  He positions the ties around each cut and ties it tightly, making a tourniquet, before rushing back down the stairs to the dispatcher.

"She's still breathing but you need to hurry.  I don't know how much longer she can survive," he tells the dispatcher, breathlessly.  The anxiety and fear are beginning to take over.  Chris doesn't know how much longer he can put on a show.  All he wants to do is break down and scream.  Curse God for continuing to punish him and take all that he loves away.

"We are on our way sir.  Has she ever cut her wrists before?"

Chris is hesitant.  He doesn't want to breach her trust in him but he knows that he needs to give all the information he can to those trying to help her.  "Y-yes.  Once before.  Right after we met."

The memory of that day still haunts Chris.  Scarlet was only his second love and he didn't know how to deal with the ups and downs of an adult relationship.  He never had issues with Laura so dealing with the emotions of Scarlet was out of his comfort zone.

"Has your wife been having issues lately that may have led to this?"

# Avance

"Umm, yes, I guess.  We were in a bad accident a few weeks ago and then we had some weird things happen prior to that.  My wife wanted to move back home but I won't listen to her...where are you guys?"  *Dammit, why didn't I listen to her?  This is all my fucking fault.  I'm killing my wife by being stubborn.*

"Sir, can you hear the sirens?  We are just down the road."

Chris listens and can hear the faint sound of sirens.  "Yes, I can hear them."  Chris breathes a sigh of relief.  Help was close and soon, his wife would be in good hands.

"Just stay on the line with me, sir; don't hang up until I tell you to."

The new little puppy stands in the corner of the kitchen, whimpering.  Chris almost forgot about that little thing for a moment.  Not only is the puppy in a new environment away from its siblings, but now there is anxiety and stress and fear circling the home.  No wonder why the puppy is whining instead of roaming.

"I won't hang up but I really need to get to my wife."

"Sir, the ambulance is just pulling into your driveway.  Is the door unlocked?'

"Umm, yes the door's unlocked."

"Ok.  Just stay with me until they make entry sir."

The seconds tick down like hours until the paramedics walk into the door.  "Sir, I'm going to let you go now."

"Thank you," he puts the phone back on the cradle.  "She's up here," he says to the paramedics before racing up the stairs to the master bedroom.

"Please help her," he pleads as the paramedics place their gear on the floor and begin working on Scarlet.

"Sir, we need you to exit the room," the older of the two paramedics request.

"No, I'm not going anywhere.  I'm staying right here with her.  I'm her husband and I won't leave her side.  Never again will I abandon her."

"Sir, you really need a do as you're asked," a voice says from behind him.  He whips his body around and see's Deputy Faulkner standing there with the puppy—Scarlet's puppy, in his hands.

"What are you doing here?"  Chris scowls at Alexander.

"The sheriff is dispatched anytime paramedics are dispatched."

# Avance

"Oh."

"Come on Mr. Haggis. Let's step outside and let the men do their jobs." Alexander gently guides Chris out of the room—puppy still in his hand.

Chris and Deputy Faulkner walk outside. Alexander places the puppy on the grass to roam around before turning to Chris. "So, has your wife ever done something like this before?"

Chris kicks some gravel on the driveway before looking the deputy in the face. "I already answered the dispatcher and I don't know what her past has anything to do with right now."

"We need to know if this is sort of thing is normal for her so we can get her the help she needs."

"Help? Help! You don't want to help. You make situations worse. She was in a horrific accident and then you tell her that her son was the person of interest in causing that accident. Furthermore, she told you about strange things happening around here but you blew her off!" Chris pauses. "She told me she felt weird about the call and the break in but I didn't listen either. I'm the reason this happened!" Chris begins to blame himself.

"Mr. Haggis, this is no one's fault. Your wife, clearly, has been under stress and you couldn't have seen this coming."

"Yeah, well I should have. I knew that she has a low stress tolerance and I didn't take her pleas to move seriously. I brushed them off and thought that a puppy was a cure-all for her."

The paramedics come out of the house with Scarlet loaded on the stretcher. "We have to get going," one yelled as they loaded the stretcher into the back of the ambulance. "We will be taking her to Mercy General if you want to follow us."

"Let me give you a ride Mr. Haggis," Alexander offers with sincerity.

"No, I'll drive myself." Chris doesn't want to be dependent upon this person. Something about Alexander rubs him the wrong way and he really doesn't care to be near him if he doesn't need to be.

"Mr. Haggis, you don't need to be driving in your condition. Why don't you accept my help?"

"Fine, but I don't know how I'll get home and who will be here for the children."

"Don't worry about those things. I'll take care of all of it. Just climb in the patrol car and stop worrying about everything else."

"But…what about the puppy?"

# Avance

"I'll go lock her in the bathroom so she doesn't destroy the house." Alexander chases the new pup down and gives her scratches behind the ear as he runs her inside the house. "Now you be a good little puppy and don't tear anything up," Alexander coos as he places a dirty towel on the bathroom floor for the nameless puppy to sleep on.

# CHAPTER FIFTEEN

Scarlet awakens to beeping and bright lights. *Where the hell am I? What the hell happened?* She goes to run her fingers through her hair when she notices tension on her arm. Her heart rate begins to pick up as her stomach begins to twist into knots. She's overwhelmed by fear as a moan escapes her mouth.

"Hey babe, you're awake," Chris says as her eyes adjust to her surroundings.

"W-what happened? Where am I? Why can't I move my arms?" Scarlet's unable to keep the fear out of her voice. This isn't the first time she's been scared since moving here and it probably wouldn't be the last.

"You're in the hospital. You cut your wrists and were bleeding when I found you yesterday. The hospital has you on a psych hold which is why you're hands are tied down right now."

"I-I didn't cut my wrists. Why the hell would you think I'd do something like that?" Her blood pressure is rising and her cheeks are red with anger.

"Honey, when I got home, you were in the bed with your wrists cut. You were unresponsive."

"Yeah, well I didn't do it! I can't remember what happened but I do know that I didn't do this!" Scarlet is growing angry. *How could he think I would do this to myself?*

"Well, if you didn't do this, then who did?" Chris condescendingly asks Scarlet.

"I don't know who did this but it wasn't me! Why do you act like you don't believe me?"

"Because you did this before, Scarlet, or have you forgotten?" Chris' tongue rolls with blame. He doesn't realize the difference from the past situation to now. His body is tense with the memory of her past suicide attempt.

Anger is rising; no, fury—that's the word. She's becoming furious at Chris. The past should always be just that; something left in the past to never be brought up again. Chris never wants to talk about his past but he sure as hell is always bringing up Scarlet's past—double standards.

"Get out, Chris!" Scarlet orders, trying to keep control in her voice and her actions.

Chris lets out a deep sigh. "I'm sorry Scarlet."

"I said, 'Get out!" Scarlet is losing control and is about to lose it on Chris. She's serious but he's not realizing just how serious she is.

"Why are you acting this way?" Chris looks at Scarlet with confusion spread across his face.

"Why am I acting this way? That's a stupid question Chris. You don't believe me. You never listen to me. Since we moved here, you live in your own fantasy world. I can't handle this right now," Scarlet's monitor begins to beep faster. "You have no issue bringing up MY past but you sure as hell are candid and shut off about your past. Now, you need to leave and you need to leave now. Just get out of here!" Scarlet's breathing is deep and fast. She can't seem to get enough oxygen into her lungs.

Without much choice and with hesitation, Chris rises from his seat. He goes to kiss Scarlet but thinks better of it and just turns and heads out of the room. He takes one last look back before the door closes and shakes his head.

Scarlet takes a deep, ragged breath. Tears begin to form in her eyes as her mind drifts to the past—a past that she has spent more than ten years trying to forget. A past that she's not proud of but it is what it is.

She was a new wife to a great man with a baby. She was thrown into the whirlwind of motherhood while working a full time paralegal job and life was hectic. The baby kept her up most nights and she dragged her feet at work and was making mistake after mistake. It wasn't long before the lawyers were looking to remove her from her position.

Something had to give and she didn't know what. She loved her husband and his, their baby boy. She couldn't fathom life without them but she loved her job too. There seemed to be no choice feasible to her because she wasn't willing to give up her family or her career.

Scarlet had felt lost—as if her world were coming to an end. She didn't realize that marrying someone with a baby would force her into making an almost impossible decision. Not seeing any way out, Scarlet had gone into their bathroom in their first apartment and removed the blade from her razor and slit both of her wrists.

Scarlet shakes her head. Remembering the past was too hard for her. She had overcome that and swore that she would never do something that stupid again. She had vowed it to her therapist, psychiatrist and her husband. Furthermore, it wasn't going to be a broken promise. She was determined to keep, or at least had been determined, to keep it.

. Yes, she's had several thoughts of ending it all since moving to Greenwich, but she's never acted upon them nor has she ever talked to anyone about those feelings. Little does Chris know, she's lived years without a single thought of ending her life, not since James was born. That is, until they moved here.

*What the hell happened? I remember locking myself in the bathroom and refusing to come out because the kids were taking forever to get ready for school and the stress of dealing with that just got the best of me and I needed alone time.*

*Chris took the kids to school and then…there was a noise. It sounded like someone was walking in the kitchen. I remember opening the door and calling out thinking that Chris had come back because one of the kids forgot something but I didn't get a response.*

# Avance

*I walked down the stairs and that's when I...oh my god, I saw him—the person that had been tormenting us.*

Her mind becomes foggy and she can't remember much after seeing the individual in her kitchen. She wants to remember but something is blocking that memory. *What the hell is wrong with me?*

"Mrs. Haggis?" a male voice pulls her from her thoughts.

"Yes?"

"I don't know if you remember me. I'm Deputy Alexander Faulkner."

"I remember you," she says, rolling her eyes, as if Alexander would be *that* easy to forget. The disdain that she feels for this man is indescribable. "What the hell do you want?"

"Ma'am, I know that you weren't happy with the evidence against your son and, yes, that case is still open and under investigation but I would like to talk about this incident. The incident that landed you back in a hospital bed." Alexander's eyes look genuinely sincere.

"Why do you care? It's not like you're going to believe a damn word I say so why does it matter?" Scarlet is still angry at Chris. If Chris didn't believe her, then why would Alexander believe her?

"Why wouldn't I believe what you say? Are you planning on lying to me or something?" Alexander gives her a half smile, trying to make light of the awkward situation.

"Why does it matter? My husband didn't believe me and you won't either."

"Try me." Alexander's eyes soften.

Scarlet tells the deputy about her past attempt at suicide, her breakdown that morning and the strange man she saw in the kitchen. "Then it just all gets foggy. I can't remember anything after that point."

Alexander finishes writing his notes and then looks up at Scarlet. His eyes hide all emotion and Scarlet is unable to decipher if he believes her or if he thinks she's as crazy as Chris does.

"You don't believe me, do you?" Her eyes focus on her lap. Butterflies dance in her belly as nerves reap havoc on her.

"I didn't say that. What makes you think that?"

"Because it sounds like something out of the movies. Something that isn't believable." Scarlet confesses, staring at her hands.

"Well, it sounds far-fetched, I'll give you that, but it does sound plausible and something that I will definitely look into. Now, can you explain to me all the things that have happened to you and your family since your arrival here?"

"Why does it matter? You can't or won't do anything. Look, I'm really tired and I just want to go to sleep if you don't mind." Scarlet turns her head to the side, away from Alexander.

The deputy, growing frustrated, rises from his seat and walks to the door. Just before exiting, he turns and looks at Scarlet. "If you don't help me, I can't help you. Things aren't adding up and nothing makes sense. I can't solve this if you won't talk to me." He turns and heads out the door.

*No one believes me so what makes him any different?* Scarlet attempt to roll over, but with her hands tied down that isn't possible. She plops her head back and closes her eyes.

# CHAPTER SIXTEEN

Scarlet was released three days later, cleared of any mental defect. When they pull into the driveway, she is greeted by a tiny little salt and pepper puppy. "Well, who's this?"

"It's a puppy, Mommy," Audrey yells. "Daddy bought her for us."

"Did he now? Well, what's her name?" Scarlet asks as she bends down to pet the puppy.

"We decided to wait until you came home and let you name her," Chris has a shit-eating grin on his face. He knew that he just scored kudo points with Scarlet.

"Well, I think she looks a little smoky and ashy. Why don't we call her Ash?"

"I think that fits her perfectly. Ash it is." Chris agrees with his wife—more kudo points.

"Yeah, our puppy's name is Ash, James," Suzanne yells, Audrey following behind her.

"You can't call her poop eater anymore," Audrey screams.

Scarlet laughs, "those girls crack me up." Scarlet looks at Chris about letting James call the puppy poop-eater.

Chris shrugs his shoulders. "Yea, they are goobers. Why don't we get you inside and comfortable," Chris takes her hand and begins to lead her to the front door.

The Haggis home damn near fell apart while she was away. Dishes were piled in the sink and the laundry room was full of dirty clothes that needed washed, ironed and put away. "Ugh, I think I want to go back to the hospital where I had no responsibilities," Scarlet half-heartedly jokes.

"Sorry, Mom, it was so hard to keep up with everything that we didn't get to your work," Charlie says as he bends down and starts to pick up the younger kids' toys. "I'll help you in the house instead of going out with Dad."

A smile spreads across Scarlet's face. "No honey, you go work with your dad. I'll send the younger three outside to play and I'll get this house whipped into shape before dinner time."

"Are you sure, Mom? I don't mind staying in here and helping you. I mean, the house is quite the mess," Charlie makes certain that she's okay with cleaning the house on her own.

"Thank sweetie, but I have this. This is my domain and I can get this mess under control faster by myself than with help. But thank you son," she pats his shoulder, proud of the man he's turning into.

The kids head out to play and Chris and Charlie head out to the field. Scarlet starts from the quickest chore and works her way up from there. Once the first load of laundry is started she is able to move on to the dishes. Chris had installed a dishwasher while she was in the hospital so she just has to rinse and load. *I must thank him for this wonderful gift. Gift? When the hell did a dishwasher turn into a gift for me?*

She presses the start button and heads to the living room for tidying up before making her way up the stairs to the second floor. *My god the girls' room is a disaster area. What the hell happened here? Did a tornado touch down or something?*

# Avance

The girls' room took Scarlet the longest to clean up because every toy they owned just happened to puke from the toy box. She will never understand how two girls as little as them can make such a large mess.

The last room on her list is the master bedroom. To her surprise, the room isn't as messy as she had imagined it to be. The sheets needed stripping and Chris' clothes needed to be picked up and put in the hamper. *I will never understand that man. He tosses his dirty clothes on the floor NEXT to the hamper. Just a couple more inches and they would land directly where they are supposed to be at.* She shakes her head as she picks up the clothes.

Scarlet drops to her knees to look under the bed for more of Chris' dirty clothes that didn't make it to the laundry basket. *Surely a stray sock or two ended up under here.* However, all Scarlet finds in a wash cloth that doesn't match anything she owns. She reaches under the bed and picks it up. As she's pulling it out, she catches a slight odor from it. A wave of nausea hits her as memories she'd suppressed begin to flood to the forefront of her brain.

*I was lying on the bed, crying. The kids were being unbearable and Chris was shaking everything off instead of seeing the turmoil I was in. I locked the bedroom door and just lay on the bed—alone.*

# Twisted Destiny

*Chris took the kids to school because I refused to open the door or even talk to him for that matter. Life was hard for me and I just needed a time out.*

*Chris hadn't been gone for long when I heard someone downstairs. I called out thinking that Chris had come back because one of the kids forgot something they needed for school.*

*I circled around into the kitchen and there he was...his face. Oh, I'll never forget that face. He resembled Charlie but it couldn't have been Charlie. Charlie had left with Chris and the other kids.*

*His eyes were evil—like shark eyes. He didn't even look human. His face was like my Charlie's face but...but slightly disfigured; like he had been burned.*

*"Hello intruder," he said to me. Oh his words were so callous—definitely not Charlie. Charlie doesn't have a mean bone in his body. A menacing tone escaped his voice as he stared at me...evil intent behind those eyes. What did he mean by 'intruder?'*

*"What do you want?" I finally managed to utter to him but he just grinned at me like I knew what he wanted.*

*He stepped quickly to me and I ran. I ran as fast as I could to my bedroom but he was on me;*

# Avance

*right at my heels. Before I could lock the door,
he was in the room—a rag in his hand.*

*I tried to scream, though I don't know what
screaming would have done for me considering
no one would've heard. The rag presses
against my mouth and I became sleepy with
every breath I took.*

Scarlet sits on the bed. Her memories stop
there and don't resume again until she awakens
in the hospital. Tears stream down her cheeks
as she remembers the fear she felt.

Anger is filling him like a boiling pot of water.
How far does he have to go before those
outsiders leave? Surely they would have left
after the attack on the mom, but he was
mistaken. He brought her to the brink of death
but maybe he'll have to bring her all the way to
death before they'll get the hint.

His mind drifts back to the morning that he
attacked her. The morning that he thought for
sure would be the family's last morning in the
farm house. How could he have thought that
they would continue to stay even though their
lives were in danger? He's not sure whether to
tip his hat to her for sticking it out or whether he
should be livid.

# Twisted Destiny

*It was easy for me to do what I had to do to Scarlet. I watched as all the kids piled in the car for their father to take them to school. Who would've thought that the kids would be the one thing that made it easy for me to get her alone?*

*I crept in through the unlocked door. I grabbed the chloroform soaked rag from my pocket and was about to make my way up the stairs when my prey—Scarlet—came to me. Half surprised, I almost jumped but I kept myself in control. How could I show her that she startled me? That would be like a bear showing fear when a deer sneaks up on him.*

*I began to walk toward her but she turned and ran. I sighed but pursued her anyways. She made it to the master bedroom where, just a few months ago, I had the pleasure of ending the life of her father-in-law.*

*She didn't have a chance. I was in the room and moving toward her with my chloroform-soaked rag. I dropped it over her mouth and, in moments, she was passed out and limp over my arm.*

*I positioned her on the bed and made my way into the bathroom. I disassembled her razor and, with the medical records I had obtained, I slit her wrists as she did many years ago. The way the razor sliced through her veins wasn't like a knife through butter. It was jagged and rough—smooth was not going to happen with a dull and very worn razor.*

He can barely contain the excitement rising from within him. Thinking about that day makes his heart beat faster and his body tingles with pure joy. Yes, he will have to up the ante if he wants them to leave. Near death didn't cut it. No—it will have to be death. Death is the only thing that will draw that family out and away from what is rightfully his.

# CHAPTER SEVENTEEN

Scarlet pushes the thoughts of the stranger out of her mind. Who would believe her anyway? Her husband thinks she's looney tunes bonkers and the sheriff thinks her eldest son is some sort of psychopath who's trying to kill his entire family—himself included.

Yes, it's better to just keep her thoughts to herself and her memories. She must dig through and solve this stalking incident herself. She doesn't even know where to begin. Maybe with Chris' sister she knew nothing about until just a few weeks ago? What about Charlie's mom? Did she even know the mom's name? What happened to her? Why doesn't she have

# Avance

Charlie or at least pay child support for this child?

"Hey Scarlet, how are you doing honey?" Chris' words pulls her from her mental list of questions she needs to find the answers to.

"Hey sweetie, I'm good, just thinking. How are you? Are the plants going to yield a good supply?"

"Oh, I think they will. We've been working awfully hard and staying ahead of the game. Farming is a roll of the dice. You can have one really good season and then, the next season you're in the red. So far, I think we're in the black."

"What do you mean 'in the black?"

"In terms of finance, red is in the negative and yellow means you're breaking even. Black means you're making a profit. I know, it's weird. It should be in the green but eh, college type business people are different to say the least."

Scarlet's mind tries to process all that Chris has just explained to her but her mind is still a million light-years away. "Yeah, it's weird. I'm glad you know what you're doing and how to do it or we may end up failing at this," she pretends to have heard everything he said.

"So, do you want to go out for supper tonight? I don't want to rush you into doing everything around here since you were just released from the hospital."

*Ha! He doesn't want me doing everything around here but I just cleaned up the entire house on my first day home. I'm sure that cooking dinner wouldn't be that big of a damn deal.* "I don't know. I could just whip up a quick dinner of breakfast goodies. Pancakes, eggs and bacon aren't difficult to make and the clean-up is easy enough."

"You could but we could go out just as easy. I say let's go out."

"Fine, we can go out," she caves. "This house was a mess anyway and one less thing to do would be nice."

"Then it's settled," Chris says, kissing her cheek. "Now, let's all get ready so we can leave."

The Haggis family piles in their car and heads toward town as their stalker looks on. He already has a plan in place. He's been lurking in the woods around the property since dusk— planning and re-planning until he's gotten it perfect in his head.

# Avance

He creeps up to the house, slowly and menacingly. He drags his feet as not to leave foot prints in the dirt. He turns the knob but the door doesn't open. *Shit, it's locked. That's okay. I'll just move on to plan B.*

He pulls out a pocket knife and begins to jimmy the lock. In a small town like Greenwich, jimmying locks isn't a common place since everyone leaves their doors unlocked so it takes him longer than he had anticipated.

The knob turns and he makes entry into the home. "Yip yip yip," comes from the Haggis family pet.

"Get the hell away," he growls at the pup before kicking it across the room. Ash yelps as her body crashes into the wall. She skitters away into the corner of the bathroom to nurse her broken ego. "Fuckin' stupid ass dog!"

He walks around the living room, staring at all the family pictures. Anger begins to build within him as he takes in all the happy and smiling faces. *I didn't have a fucking Kodak childhood. I was fucking abandoned! No one wanted me. I was different and repugnant.*

He scrunches his face up in anger and jealousy before making his way up the stairs to the girls' room—his original destination. He sits on the bed and lights a smoke. He inhales a deep drag and holds it for a minute before exhaling. "God, that feels good," he says, ragged before coughing as the smoke irritates his lungs. He flicks the ashes on the floor, not caring that he's making a mess.

A few moments later, he field strips the cigarette on the floor and crushes the cherry into the carpet before placing the filter in his pocket. "Now, to get this show on the road!" He walks to the girls' dresser and begins to rummage through it. Their panty drawer was the top drawer—just the drawer he was in search of. He pulls the panties out one at a time, and raises them to his nose. He inhales deep as a menacing smile spreads across his face. "Mmmmm, pure innocence."

He pulls out his pocket knife and begins to shred the panties—one by one. He leaves them on the bed and, as if by second thought, he unzips his jeans and begins to masturbate over their mauled panties. Sweat forms across his brow and he bites his bottom lip as he begins to reach his climax. "Arrrg," escapes his throat as he ejaculates over their panties and duvet.

He exits their room with a sort of accomplishment in his step. He strolls down the hallway and into the master bedroom. He rummages through the drawers in there and finds Scarlet's intimates in her top drawer. His eyes become slanted and his demeanor changes. His soul, if you can say he has one, is filled with anger and animosity. Strength overcomes him and he shreds the panties with both hands. Rips and tears echo in the room.

Rage fills him. Rage and hatred are the only feelings that he can muster up at this point. His stomach begins to churn and roll with the stress and anxiety that flows through his veins. As if he's being controlled by something out of this world, he pulls his pants down and begins to defecate on her panties and the bed she shares with Chris. This was not part of his plan but improvising never felt so good.

He finishes the deed and wipes his ass with the duvet. He lights another smoke and inhales as he looks around at his handy work. Pleased with himself, he begins to saunter out of the room and down the stairs. As he's exiting, he sees the little pup rummaging around in the kitchen. *Fucking pets!*

His mind drifts back to the first foster home he ever lived in that had a dog. *The damned dog never quit its fucking yipping. It was some stupid ass breed that was good for nothing. I had to have been about seven years old and that fucker would always nip at my ankles.*

*One night, not long after moving in with that couple, I'd had enough of that fucker and lured him to the pond on the property. Once he had crept to the water's edge, I scooped him up.*

# Twisted Destiny

*The screeching that little shit was doing was ear piercing. In one swift movement, I dunked that fucker under the water and held him until long after he'd stopped flailing about.*

The memory puts a smile on his face. That was the first life that he'd ever taken and the adrenaline rush he received was amazing. Even for a youngster, he was addicted—addicted to the thrill of the kill.

The hideous yipping of the family's dog brings him to the present. He starts toward the puppy when she bolts. He begins to chase her but is stopped, dead in his tracks, by headlights coming up the driveway. He looks at the clock and curses himself. "I've been here for over an hour! Too fucking long and now I may not have time to escape! Stupid fool!"

He rushes out toward the back door. Praying and hoping he can get out and make it through the open field and into the orchard before the family can spot him. The door is locked and it takes him precious seconds to get it unlocked. Before he knows it, he's sprinting across the field, through the shadows of darkness. Thank God for the approaching season change or else daylight would be still streaking across the sky.

# CHAPTER EIGHTEEN

The Haggis family makes their way into their home. Nothing seems disturbed but Scarlet feels a chill of alertness spread down her spine. A pungent stench fills her nostrils as she looks up at Chris. "Oh my God, what is that smell? Did the dog poo in the house?" She looks for signs of defecation from the puppy, Ash, but finds nothing. "Where is Ash?" she asks Chris.

"I don't know. I left her in the house. Maybe she's sleeping somewhere."

The family begins to search and finds her in the laundry room, sleeping on top of the dirty clothes that Scarlet had yet to throw in the wash.

"Well, she didn't poop down here, but that smell is growing worse," Scarlet says as she still continues the search of the poop that she knows just *has* to be around there somewhere.

"Yeah, it is. Why don't we get the kids ready for bed and then we will continue to hunt down and locate the cause of the bad smell," Chris suggests as he leans in and kisses Scarlet's cheek.

Scarlet and Chris walk the girls up the stairs. The smell intensifies the closer they get to the top. "Oh my God, what the hell is that? It smells like backed up sewage or something," Scarlet pinches her nose and tries not to gag. The smell burns her nostrils and makes her eyes water.

As she goes to pass the master bedroom, she glances in and sees the horrific scene. "What the fuck!" She screams as she takes in the carnage of her bedroom.

Audrey's face gets serious. "Ah, Mommy, you said a naughty word. You have to…"

"Not now!" Scarlet cuts Audrey off, rudely.

"What the hell is going…" Chris says before looking in the room. "…what the hell?…who did this shit?" Anger replaces horror on his face. "Take the girls downstairs and call the sheriff's department."

# Avance

Scarlet stands, legs unable to move. She heard Chris but is unable to follow direction. "Scarlet!! Now! Go downstairs!"

As if a fire was lit under her ass, Scarlet ushers the children back the way they'd come. "Sit down at the counter and I'll get you guys some hot cocoa," she says as she pours milk into a pot and puts it on the stove.

"Mom, what's going on upstairs?" Charlie questions, James close at his big brother's side. They had been outside with Ash and were unaware of the horrors of the master bedroom. "And did you ever find out what that horrible smell is?" He plugs his nose as to try to ward off the vial stench.

"Umm, nothing Sweetie. Don't worry about it. Do you want some hot cocoa?" She asks as she picks up the phone and dials the sheriff's number.

"No, I don't want any cocoa. Is everything alright, Mom?" Charlie's growing frustrated.

"Charlie, just stop alright. There is nothing going on that you need to concern yourself with." Scarlet's frustration at the situation is growing. Snapping at her children isn't common place for her but her nerves are so frazzled that she can't control her emotions.

"Alright, Mom. Is there anything I can do to help you?" Charlie takes a different approach sensing his mom's mood.

"Finish the younger kids' hot cocoa and get them served please. I'm going to step outside and make a phone call." She walks out with the cordless phone that Chris had conveniently bought after she was found with her wrists slit.

She dials the number and hits the call button on the phone and, almost instantly, is connected with the dispatcher. "Yes, this is Scarlet Haggis. I need to talk to Deputy Faulkner."

"I'm sorry ma'am, but he's not in at the moment. Can I take a message?" The dispatcher seemed friendly but Scarlet didn't want to talk to anyone else and she damn sure didn't want to leave a message. She needed Alexander now.

"No, I don't think you understand. I need Deputy Faulkner right now. He's investigating some suspicious activities that have been going on here and we just had another...fiasco. Could you please get him on the line?" Agitation is radiating through every nerve in Scarlet and she doesn't even try to act nice to the dispatcher.

After a short pause and some clicking of a keyboard, the dispatcher spoke again, this time sounding annoyed. "I'm transferring you to his cell phone. If he doesn't answer, leave a message and he will get back to you at his earliest convenience." The line went silent before it began to ring again.

"Alexander Faulkner," he says as he answers the line. It's his one day off and he was enjoying a day of relaxing.

"Deputy Faulkner? This is Scarlet Haggis. Our stalker is at it again and this time...well, words can't even describe what he's done to our home."

He inhales and exhales, clearly annoyed that his only day off has now been interrupted by someone who has nothing better to do than to stalk and torment a family. "I'll be there shortly," he says before hanging up the line.

Scarlet ends the call on her end and sighs. Life has been Hell since moving to Greenwich. She doesn't want to live here anymore and, in fact, her mind is made up—she's moving back to Los Angeles as soon as possible. She loves Chris and wants to spend the rest of her life with him but she refuses to be tormented and stalked to make him happy. She shivers from an unusual cold breeze and walks back inside.

He lurks in the orchard surrounding the property. Watching as the family huddles in the kitchen and the woman talks on the phone outside. *The cops aren't going to be able to catch me. It's*

*just a waste of time;* he chuckles to himself and smiles a vindictive and sly grin.

Chris thinks he can pick and choose what he gets in life, but he can't. The issue that the stalker has is not the result of Scarlet or her children—no, it's the result of decisions made by Chris long before he met her. She, unfortunately, is just collateral damage.

He turns and walks deeper in the trees. There's nothing more that he can do tonight. It's time to retire to his room to make plans for the big finale.

# CHAPTER NINETEEN

Alexander Faulkner is good at his job. A case has never gone cold that he's worked, but then again, nothing like this has ever happened before in his county. All of the events that this person is doing is completely abnormal for this small town.

"What the hell are these guys into? What did they do back in Los Angeles?" Alexander says aloud on his way out to their farm house. He knew Chris when they were kids. Chris was two years his senior and he's certain that Chris doesn't remember him. Then again, why would he? He was too busy with his jock friends to notice anyone younger than him. The only run in they had was when he had asked Laura out on a date and Chris damn near beat his face in.

He pulls into the driveway and cuts the engine. He exhales a ragged breath before reaching for his hat and exiting his patrol car. Thoughts from the past on this farm flood his mind. His family resided not far from this farm and he would sneak around here. Things didn't add up and something was completely off at the Haggis residence. Alexander was determined to figure it out but he never found enough evidence to prove any theory he had.

"I'm sorry to call you out so late Deputy Faulkner. I wouldn't have but these pranks, if you want to call them that, are escalating and I don't feel like my family is safe anymore." Scarlet comes onto the porch.

"It's alright," he lies. "I wasn't doing anything important anyway," he says extending another lie. He was relaxing. That's important for law enforcement officers—relaxation away from the drama of disturbances and criminals. If anyone needs relaxation, it's definitely those in law enforcement.

"We haven't touched anything upstairs. In fact, aside from finding the carnage, we all retreated back to the kitchen and had bunkered down while we waited for you so we didn't disturb anything," Chris pipes in, standing just behind Scarlet.

"Thanks. What exactly happened?" Alexander grabs a snuff of Copenhagen. If he had to work tonight he wasn't going to be able to do it without some chew.

"Well, someone really needed to take a shit and did it on our bedding after he ripped all of my wife's panties," Chris explains, feeling a bit uncomfortable. "I went and checked the other rooms and I found that he had torn my daughters' panties and then, it appears that he may have jerked off on top of them." Chris slightly cringes as he explains to Alexander what he had found.

Scarlet gasps, "no....are you kidding me? He's going after our children?" Tears begin to flood her eyes. She's unable to keep them from pooling over and sliding down her cheeks.

"It's okay, baby. It's all going to be okay," Chris wraps his arms around her.

She shakes him off. "No it's fucking not! You love this damned old house more than you do your own fucking family! Why don't you get your shit figured out, Chris?!" She storms off. Heading toward the trees of the orchard, leaving both men watching her yet neither able to form words.

"Well, I'm going to go up and investigate the scene if that's alright," Alexander tips his hat to Chris before entering the residence.

"Oh yeah, that's fine. I left the lights on in both rooms or would you like me to take you there?"

"Umm, no, I'll be able to find them. I think it's best that you stay in the kitchen with the kids. Just don't leave the kitchen area just in case there's trace evidence in other parts of the house."

After retrieving his evidence case from the car, Alexander Faulkner begins to process the scene. The rooms are completely in disarray and the master bedroom reeks of shit. Being a deputy in a small town, Alexander is accustomed to shitty smells but human feces is, by far, the worst smell. *Damn, this stalker really is a psychopath. No sane person would take a dump on someone's bed and then wipe their ass with the duvet. What the fuck am I dealing with?*

He photographs everything he can before he begins to swab and dust the room. In a small town, the resources are limited. There's no calling people in to process a crime scene. When Carl and Mary Ellen were murdered, the state troopers had to be called in because the crime was far more advanced. This scene, however, is a cake walk for Alexander.

# Avance

Alexander's heart pangs when he hears the laughter of the children downstairs. He'd longed for a family but the cards were never in his favor. He's only ever pined after one woman but she never returned the feelings. She was the girl of his dreams and...well after her death some sixteen or so years ago, he just never got over it. Alexander knows that it's stupid to waste one's life on unrequited love but that's exactly what he did. He wasted his life longing after a memory of what could have been.

"Are you almost done?" Chris' voice pulls him from his flashback.

"Oh, yeah, I'm just finishing up. I bet those kids are ready for bed."

"Yeah and Scarlet hasn't come home yet so I need to get the young ones down and go out and find her."

"She's still not home? It's been a couple of hours," Alexander mentions as he places the soiled duvet from the master bedroom in the large evidence bag.

"Yeah, I'm getting a bit worried. She doesn't really know the area and I'm afraid she could be lost or have gotten hurt or something."

"Yeah, I can understand that. Let me get these things into the patrol car and secured and I'll sweep the orchards with you. She's probably fine, but it's better to be safe than sorry."

"Thank you. I appreciate it. She's so jittery and jumpy most of the time that I'm actually surprised that she left in the dark by herself."

"Well, can you blame her? I mean, I don't know what your life was like back in LA and I don't really care to know the details but since you guys have moved out here, it's been a one ringed circus for her. Have you thought about the toll this puts on her?" Alexander asks, getting a little too personal with Chris.

"Yeah, it's been Hell here but I don't think that I asked for your input on my marriage."

Alexander wants to yell at Chris. He wants to make him understand that he has everything a man could ask for and he's pissing it away by staying here in Greenwich. Alexander wants to tell him all of that and more, but he doesn't. "You're right. I shouldn't give my two cents to your situation. I'm going to go search the orchards." Alexander stomps off in search of Chris' missing wife. The man treats Alexander like crap but he still has a job to do and an oath to maintain.

# CHAPTER TWENTY

Scarlet walks through the trees, her anger is raging full throttle within her and Chris just doesn't understand. She needs to distance herself from the situation before she completely blows up. Chris thought that the move here would be good for his family, especially the children. No gangs or smog or bad influences to steer them off course, but he doesn't see that this—this situation is unhealthy for her and the kids.

They need to get back to Los Angeles—to safety. Who would have ever imagined calling Los Angeles safe? Scarlet knows the dangers of a big city but she's also discovering the dangers of a small town. Out here, the police can't get to them soon enough in the event of an emergency. Out here, there are no hourly patrols; hell, there aren't even daily patrols.

Scarlet is definitely not staying around Greenwich anymore. Regardless of what Chris wants, she's packing her kids up and heading back to Los Angeles as soon as she gets back to the farmhouse. *I can get all of our things packed and purchase five plane tickets for the first flight out tomorrow. I'm sure I'll be able to get my job back and I can rent a three bedroom apartment until I can find a house.*

With Scarlet's plan in place, she begins to shiver as the cold wind chills her bones. Very well enough because she needs to get back and make arrangements for a trip halfway across the country. She turns to head back when a glowing red light catches her eye. "Hello? Is anyone there?" Scarlet calls out into the darkness. No response. Scarlet shrugs her shoulders and wraps her arms around her chest. She continues on her path back home when heavy footsteps stop her dead in her tracks.

"W-who's there?" Scarlet's voice cracks with anxiety. Her heart is racing and she feels the urge to flee. Her fight or flight response is kicking in and she wants to flee but her legs are failing her and there is no way she wants to fight.

# Avance

Scarlet regains some self-control and uncrosses her arms. "Quit being a chicken shit and show yourself, you coward." Strength overcomes her and it feels great. Yes, she's still anxious but she's not allowing her fear to control her.

Beads of sweat form along her neck as she waits for a response. Nothing. Not a damn sound anywhere. "Just like I thought; a damn coward hiding in the cover of darkness," Scarlet huffs in triumph.

She turns to head home and is startled by a figure standing only mere feet from her. The figure raises his hand to his face and inhales. The cherry of the cigarettes lights up red with the inhalation. Scarlet's stomach begins to churn as liquid warmth fills her mouth. The urge to vomit is great. Her anxiety is in full control and she can't even conjugate any words.

The stranger exhales the smoke and chuckles. "So, I'm a coward, eh? I'm a chicken shit? Would a coward confront you? Would a chicken shit show his face?" He laughs a menacing laugh before tossing his cigarette to the ground and crushing it. "Well, cat got your tongue, Bitch?"

Before she knows it, Scarlet is turning around and running further into the orchard—deeper than she's ever been before. Her chest is burning as she quickly inhales and exhales oxygen into her lungs. She hasn't run in years and this time, she's in for the run of her life. She's scared shitless. *Who is he? What does he want? Will I survive his attack this time?* So many thoughts race through Scarlet's head. So many emotions flow through her veins; fear, anxiety and anger.

She has no clue where's she's headed or which direction she's facing as she's taken many twists and turns along the way. All she knows is she needs to find safety and soon. She can hear her stalker's heavy footsteps behind her over the thumping of her rapidly beating heart.

Just as she sees a clearing ahead of her, just within footsteps, strong arms wrap around her waist and a sharp pain forms in her right side. "HEEELLLLP!" she manages to scream before his hand wraps around her mouth and another sharp pain engulfs her. Scarlet's body is cringing with pain. Darkness is engulfing her. The figure creeps into her line of vision and opens his mouth.

"I told you to leave. Now you will suffer." Scarlet shudders with fear before the darkness takes her.

# CHAPTER TWENTY-ONE

Alexander Faulkner begins his search for Scarlet leaving Chris behind. It's probably for the best considering he'd overstepped his boundary and inputted his two cents where it didn't belong. Alexander is, now, certain that Chris doesn't remember him. Then again, why would he? Alexander had only merely watched Chris from a distance. He knew Chris but no way did Chris know him.

Alexander begins to think about the last time anyone in this town had seen Chris. It was December and there was snow littering the soil. The storm had been bad that year and everyone worried that they wouldn't survive. She was very much pregnant and rumors were spreading like wild fire. Who was the father? Did she even know who the father was? She'd never been seen with anyone. How could the pregnancy possibly happen?

Yes, everyone had their own theory regarding each question but no one had the theory that Alexander had. He tried sharing his theory once and was ridiculed by his best friend, Kyle McInter. Never again did he voice his opinion but he couldn't shake it. He just knew that his theory fit and it was the truth but, with no evidence, he couldn't prove it.

"HEELLLP!" Alexander heard Scarlet scream. It was an ear piercing scream that sent chills down his spine. She was in trouble and he had to find her—save her. He turned to his left, where the scream originated from, and took off at a dead run. He was pushing branches back and jumping over trenches. One scream; she only screamed once. *Where is she? Why isn't she screaming anymore?* "Scarlet?" He hollers out, hoping and praying for a response.

"Scarlet, it's Deputy Faulkner. If you can hear me, call out!" His stomach is doing flip flops. He wants so badly for her to answer him, but there is nothing. The only sounds he hears are the wind blowing between the trees and leaves blowing around on the ground. An owl in the distance is the only living thing he hears.

# Avance

He points his flashlight along the ground, looking for any evidence that Scarlet is nearby. He knows what he heard and he knows it wasn't a figment of his imagination. *Where the hell is she?*

About two yards in front of Alexander, he sees her, lying motionless on the ground and covered in blood. He races over the uneven ground and kneels down by her side. "Scarlet? Scarlet, can you hear me?" He asks as he scans the trees, looking for anything or anyone lurking in the shadows. "Scarlet, can you hear me?" Alexander asks again as he places his flashlight on the ground and removes his jacket and places it over Scarlet's body.

Alexander gets on his radio and calls in for assistance and medical support. "Tonya," he calls to the dispatcher. "I need back up and medical support at the old Haggis Farm. We have a thirty-something year old woman with apparent stab wounds, unconscious in the orchards surrounding the property. I'm about one hundred yards southeast of the residence."

"Back up and medical support are in route," Tonya says, allowing Alexander to breathe a sigh of relief. However, his relief is short lived when he hears footsteps coming from behind him. He draws his service weapon and retrieves his flashlight. Kneeling down, he spins around with the flashlight in his left hand, under his armed, right hand. "Freeze," he orders the approaching figure. His heart is racing and sweat is forming along his upper lip and around his neck. His finger's on the trigger, twitching with anticipation.

# CHAPTER TWENTY-TWO

"Hey whoa man, don't shoot," Chris says, his hands up above his head. "What's going on?" Chris questions, confused and a bit scared.

Alexander holsters his firearm and rises from his position. He takes a few strides toward Chris. "Chris, your wife's been injured," he starts, trying to spare him how badly she'd been injured. "I'm waiting for back up and medical transport for her." Alexander has sympathy for Chris. He regrets what he said before he left the farmhouse. If he knew then what he knows now, he would've kept his trap shut.

"What do you mean injured? What the fuck happened?" Chris yells, his voice shakes with both anger and worry. Anger at the situation and worry about his wife—again. Poor Scarlet just can't seem to catch a break. Chris tries to look past Alexander but he won't get out of his way.

"Chris, she's been stabbed. I don't know by whom or how long ago it happened or how bad her injury is, but she's unconscious." Alexander wishes his back up would arrive. He hates being out here alone with an injured victim, her emotional spouse and a crazed stalker—turned psychotic, on the loose.

Chris starts to walk toward Scarlet. Alexander holds his arm out to stop him. "You don't want to go over there. I want to keep the scene as clean as I can for evidence."

"You better get your fucking hands off of me. I don't give a rat's ass if you're law enforcement, I'll break your damn arm in two to get to my wife," Chris' face turns red with anger.

Alexander doesn't tolerate people threatening him, but he makes an exception this time. "Look, I'll show you to her but you can't go moving around the area. Stay in one place so we can salvage any evidence that the attacker may have left behind," Alexander explains as he steps back and allows Chris access to his wife.

Chris kneels down to Scarlet and strokes her hair. "Oh baby, what the hell happened?" Tears begin to slide down his cheek as he hovers above his beautiful wife. She's lying on the ground with her head to one side and her legs resting the opposite direction. "I'll find you, you fucking son-of-a-bitch," Chris yells through the darkness. He hoped and prayed like hell the attacker was out there. He hoped he heard him. He would make good on his promise.

"Hey man, the paramedics are here," Alexander places his hand on Chris' shoulder. "You need to move out of the way so they can tend to your wife."

Chris ignores Alexander. Alexander, trying to remain understanding and compassionate toward him, leans down to his level. "Chris, we need to let the paramedics do their job so they can save Scarlet's life."

That seems to get to Chris. He rises up but his pain and sorrow is quickly replaced with anger and rage. "I fucking told you that my son had nothing to do with the car accident but you wasted all your energy investigating my family. What the fuck have you been doing to find out who's doing this to our family? Have you even got another suspect? Why don't you get off your ass and do your fucking job?" Chris yells at Alexander while the paramedics load Scarlet on the gurney and take off out of the orchard.

Alexander is beginning to lose his self-composure. Chris' attitude toward the whole situation is getting under his skin. He's not the only one to blame for all of this. "Listen, I'm about to lose my patience with you! I'm not the only one to blame here. Something is going on, that's for sure, and no, Charlie is no longer a suspect, but you need to start being honest with me and your damn self for that matter."

"What the fuck is that supposed to mean?" Chris questions as he paces around.

"It means that you aren't being honest with me or yourself. It means that there is something in your closet that you aren't telling anyone and that's making solving this damned case harder, if not impossible." Alexander is getting angry. He wants to solve this mystery but Chris is not being forthcoming and it's frustrating.

Chris pauses. Can he tell Alexander what's going on? Can he confess his past transgressions? It's a secret he's carried since before Charlie was born and he never imagined telling anyone his secret. The world would frown at what he'd done. What he'd done was, for the most part, illegal and immoral. Furthermore, what he's done affects his son. If his secret gets out in a small town like this, Charlie's life will be permanently changed.

# Avance

"So are you going to tell me what the fuck is going on here so I can help your family or are you going to continue to put them in harm's way to continue to protect yourself?" Alexander is growing impatient with Chris. He's never seen such a coward before.

"I want to go to the hospital with my wife," Chris snaps as he begins to walk toward the house. "I have to get my kids up."

Alexander sighs. *This man is going to be the death of me.* "Let me call Nancy Sherpa to come watch the kids. I'll drive you to Mercy General Hospital. You don't need to be driving in your condition and the kids don't need to be drug out this late," Alexander follows behind Chris, kicking up dirt as he drags his feet.

"That's not necessary. I can take care of myself and my family without anyone's help. I'm not helpless." Chris stops and faces Alexander. His face is contorted with disdain.

"Look, I'm not saying you're helpless. All I'm saying is that the kids don't need to be drug out this late and you need a support system. That's all," Alexander hold his hands up in surrender.

Chris sighs. "You're right. Let's go."

# CHAPTER TWENTY-THREE

Chris is sitting in the waiting room while Scarlet undergoes surgery. The doctor explained that she had some major internal bleeding and her spleen may have been ruptured as a result. His mind is racing with so many thoughts. *What if she dies? Why didn't I just sell the property and move back to L.A.? How will I go on without her?* These thoughts haunt every part of his consciousness. He's made mistakes before but none this detrimental.

"Here," Pastor Ned Sherpa says, handing Chris a cup of coffee. "I'm not sure how good it is but it's hot and should help calm your nerves."

# Avance

Chris accepts the cup but doesn't sip. His mind is too clustered to think about drinking or eating anything and his stomach would revolt to anything being introduced. "Thank you, Ned."

Alexander comes in the room and sits next to Chris. "I just got an update. They will be a few more hours. There was some extensive damage and they are repairing it now. Scarlet is stable and they believe that the surgery will be successful."

"Thanks," Chris says without making eye contact with Alexander. Alexander makes Chris angry and he's not exactly sure why. *Did I know him in high school? Did we have issues back then?* So many questions race through Chris' mind as he tries to discover why he holds so much hostility towards the deputy.

"You're welcome. I'm going to head back to the orchard and help look for evidence. If you need me, you have my cell phone," he says to both Chris and Ned.

"Thank you Alexander," Ned says standing up to shake his hand. "We will phone you if there are any updates."

"Yeah, thanks deputy. If you find anything, please keep us informed." Chris stands to shake Alexander's hand.

\*\*\*

Alexander arrives at the property with the state troopers. The crimes had escalated to the point that the Sheriff's department is no longer equipped to handle the matter. Alexander hated having to make that call but with another Haggis life in danger, he had no choice. "Hey Bill," Alexander says to William Calhoun, the lead investigator for the Nebraska State Troopers.

"Hey Alex, I guess we just can't get away from this property, eh?" Bill was the lead investigator for the murders that occurred here just a few months ago and here he was back for an attempted murder. It still pissed him off that he never figured out who murdered Mary Ellen and Carl Haggis.

"This property is going to be the death of my career. I swear, I can't get an angle on this perpetrator and Chris Haggis is not very cooperative," Alexander says, looking at the little yellow number tabs indicating where evidence is that needs to be photographed and bagged. He can't get the image of Mary Ellen with her throat slit and Carl with his knee caps blown off out of his head. It was the most grisly sight he'd ever seen and one he won't ever forget.

Bill shakes his head. "Well, he's going to have to be more cooperative if we plan on solving this thing. I hate that his parents' case is still unsolved. Do you think the two are related?"

# Avance

Alexander looks at Bill, confusion washing over his face. "Why would we assume the two weren't related? The parents were gruesomely murdered here just a few months ago and then when Chris and his family move in, the stalking starts up with Scarlet becoming the stalker's prime target. How can these two cases not be interlinked?"

"For a town this size, it would be extremely rare for two different perps but it's still possible. I've seen less likely things happen in my lifetime," Bill says as the two begin to walk through the orchard looking at all the evidence, or lack thereof, that was left behind.

"Yeah, but this is related. I'm sure of it. Now, we just need to figure out why so we can find the who," Alex points out. How could this not be related? No one else in town is being stalked or harassed. "We need to find out what skeletons the Haggis family is hiding in their closet. Someone is pissed off as hell at them and this won't end until we find out what they're hiding."

"Has Chris given you any information?" Bill asks as he shines his flashlight over the ground.

"No. He's not opening up about anything and it's starting to piss me off. If he would just talk we might be able to solve this case before anyone else gets hurt," Alexander shines his flashlight around as well. Not really sure what he's looking for but looking nonetheless.

"Well, are any of the Haggis family smokers?" Bill asks bending down next to a crushed cigarette.

"No, not a single one of them," Alexander says, hopeful that this cigarette is from the killer.

"Well then, we might have a strong lead." Bill bags the crushed cigarette in an evidence bags and hands it off to a crime scene investigator. "Get this to the lab ASAP. I want a DNA profile from it in the next forty-eight hours."

# CHAPTER TWENTY-FOUR

He limps in the front door; winded and exhausted. Scarlet's fighting took a lot out of him and the Sheriff's unexpected arrival sent his heart racing. Surely, he thought he was caught and that was the end of all of his years of planning and executing.

He turns the bathroom light on and checks his face. Three scratches slice through the left side of his face where the bitch swatted at him. "Fucking bitch," he says as he runs his fingers along the marks.

His testes throb as he starts to unbuckle his belt and unzip his jeans. The bitch grabbed his junk with one hand and squeezed and twisted as hard as she could before he finally hit her in the head with a rock.  His testicles and penis were purple and swollen.  "Goddammit.  She's a ruthless fucking bitch," he zips his pants up and limps to the kitchen for something frozen to place over his manhood.

He settles down in the chair in the living room and places a package of meat over his junk and clicks on the television.  His mind is racing.  This was not the night he'd expected.  He was hiding out in the orchard waiting to see the outcome of the little "gift" he'd left in the bedrooms.  He wanted to see what would transpire.  He was in the first row of trees when Scarlet blew her top with Chris and the deputy.

When she began walking toward the orchard— toward him, a smile formed across his face.  Oh he couldn't believe that she was walking toward him.  The prey was coming to her own slaughter.  He quickly started moving further into the orchard; away from prying eyes.  *Could this be true?  Was she really walking straight toward me?*

A smile creeps along his face as he remembers the excitement he felt as his brain realized that, yes indeed, she was walking straight toward him.  He hurriedly thought out a plan and hoped it would work.  He wasn't used to doing things on a whim but he didn't have time to devise an elaborate plan.

He watched her for the duration of her time in the orchard. He heard her curses and felt her anger. When she had calmed down and was heading back to the house, that's when he made his move. He made a rustling noise to stop her in her tracks and then, when she thought she was brave enough to confront him, he pounced. Oh the joy he felt as he stuck the knife into her side—not once but twice. It slid through skin and flesh like butter.

When she scratched him and grabbed his family jewels, he almost shrieked in pain but he bit his tongue—literally. He found a rock on the ground and beat her upside her head. Without a sound, she was knocked out. Maybe, just maybe, he left her dead or, at best, brain damaged. A smile spreads over his face when the thought of her dead crosses his mind. *Oh, that would be better than I ever could have hoped for.*

# CHAPTER TWENTY-FIVE

Chris has been at the hospital for nearly twenty-four hours. Scarlet's surgery was over eight hours long. She's been in ICU for nearly twelve hours and has yet to regain consciousness. The doctors explained that she had some trauma to her brain and that there was nothing more they could do for her but wait and see.

Chris hated the waiting game but he wasn't alone. Pastor Ned Sherpa hadn't left the hospital. In fact, Chris was sure he was still sitting in the waiting room. Ned's wife, Nancy, was taking care of the kids. Last he'd heard, the kids were doing well and Nancy had cleaned up the mess from the night before. Ned called the church and was having a schedule made up so someone was with the kids all the time and someone was always at the hospital. *We wouldn't have this support if we were still in L.A. However, I suppose we wouldn't be in this situation if we had stayed.*

Chris sighs at the thought. He hates to admit it but Scarlet was right. They needed to go back home. It was far safer for them in Los Angeles than it was in this little town. Everything had changed and, unfortunately, not for the better. "Oh Scarlet, I'm so sorry I didn't listen to you. Baby, if you wake up, I promise we will move back to Los Angeles as soon as possible. I don't want to lose you." Chris is overcome with emotions. He always knew he loved Scarlet but he didn't know just how much until now. He lost one true love, and he would be damned if he lost another woman he loved.

"How are you doing, Chris," Ned says as he hands him a cup of coffee. "Milk with three sugars."

"Thanks Ned. I'm doing okay. I just wish Scarlet would wake up." Chris sighs as he sips the coffee.

"All in God's time. You know He knows what our future holds and we just have to have faith that He will protect us and give us strength."

"Yeah, well God hasn't been so nice to me. He seems to think that I'm a mistake and gives me hardships after hardships."

Ned Sherpa, a man of God, has heard Chris' complaints from many parishioners. It's not uncommon for people, even Christian people, to lose faith in God when bad things begin to happen to them. "Chris, when bad things happen, we tend to forget all the good things that God has given us. All you're thinking about is your parents' death or the attacks on Scarlet or the accident your family was in," he says, as he pulls up the second chair in the room and takes a seat. "But you forget the gorgeous children that God has given you and the years of marriage to the woman you love. How about the means to support that family and all the towns folk that have rallied to support and help your family?"

Chris nods his head but keeps his mouth shut. He doesn't want to rock the boat with Ned by telling him that he doesn't believe in his God and he hasn't in quite some time. He was an atrocity to God—a mistake. How would his father have put it? Oh yeah, an abomination. Chris was not Godly nor has he been a Godly man since the day he became one with Laura. "I hear ya," is all that he could muster to respond to Ned. He hoped it was enough to pacify the old pastor.

"The whole town is praying for Scarlet. Trust in prayer and in God. Find some peace in knowing that His miracles are bigger than anything man can do."

"I know," Chris lies.

"Would you like some breakfast? Clarissa Gleeson has brought down some eggs, bacon and biscuits and she even thought to include some better tasting coffee," Ned explains with a half-smile forming on his weary face.

"I could go for a bite to eat, but I don't want to leave Scarlet's side. What if she wakes up and I'm not here? Or, God forbid what if she takes a turn for the worst and I'm in another room stuffing my face full of food and coffee?" Chris is anxious. He knows that he needs sustenance but fears leaving his wife. Every time he leaves her, something horrible happens to her.

"Let me talk to nurse Amy and see if we can't pull some strings and bring some food in here," Ned exclaims as he rises and exits the room in search of the nurse.

"Thank goodness he left," Chris says to Scarlet as he strokes her hand. "I don't know if I had the strength to continue to listen to him talk about God for one more second." He kisses her hand while he begins to devise a plan to move his family back to Los Angeles. He knows that he has to get them back to safety. What he thought would be the best time of their lives and the safest place to live has turned out to be the worst decision he'd ever made, aside from leaving Laura and their other son behind.

Avance

# CHAPTER TWENTY-SIX

Charlie comes downstairs earlier than normal. He knows that Nancy and Clarissa have been running ragged trying to keep their previous engagements as well as taking care of him and his younger siblings. It's time for him to step up and be the man of the house while his dad is at the hospital with his mom.

He quietly begins to cook up a healthy breakfast for the kids. He grabs eggs, cheese, bacon and bread from the fridge and gets to work. He's watched his mom cook many times before so he knows the order in which to start things. The pan is heating for the bacon as he cuts a pound of it in half and begins placing it in the warm skillet.

He's on a roll until the bacon begins to spit and splatter grease all over the place. "Shit, ouch, that shit smarts!" He says as he jumps back from the skillet as he attempts to turn over a piece of overly done bacon.

"Are we having a bit of trouble?" Clarissa Gleeson says from behind him. Her and Nancy take alternate days coming over and today is her day. Nancy was supposed to stay the night last night with the kids but she had an emergency.

"Yeah, this bacon hates me," Charlie says as he looks over his shoulder at her. His breath catches when he sees Charlotte, her daughter, standing beside her mother.

"Bacon hates everyone, Sweetie. The longer you cook it the more you learn to outsmart all its spits of grease. Here, let me take over," she wraps an apron around her waist and takes the fork from Charlie. "Why don't you go wake your siblings up and help them get dressed? I'll get breakfast whipped up in a jiffy."

Charlie nods to the women in the kitchen and makes his way back upstairs to wake his siblings up. They were wound pretty tight last night when he and Mrs. Sherpa put them to bed. It took several stories and multiple drinks of water before they finally zonked out. Mrs.

# Avance

Sherpa stayed until they were out but she had an emergency with a church member and needed to leave.

Suzanne and Audrey were snuggled up in the same bed. Since Scarlet was attacked and Chris spent all day and night at the hospital, the girls tend to sleep together. Charlie didn't mind that they did that because he knew that it made the girls feel safe and secure. "Hey sleepy heads. It's time to rise and shine. Breakfast will be ready in a few so you two need to get up," he slightly sings to his younger siblings as he flicks the light on.

"But I don't wanna," Audrey protests and draws the blankets over her head.

"Yeah, me either!" Suzanne concurs as she rolls over on her belly and sticks her head under the pillow.

"I know, I know. It's too damn early to be up but it's Friday and tomorrow you girls get to sleep in."

"Ohhh, you said a bad word," Suzanne tattles as she lifts her head from beneath the pillow.

"Yeah, you said a bad word. You need to put a nickel in the swear jar," Audrey pipes in.

"Fine, I'll put a nickel in the swear jar but you two have to get up and get dressed," he compromises as he begins to pull out clothes for each of the girls to wear. "Now, get dressed while I go wake James up," he says over his shoulder as he walks out of the room.

"James," Charlie says as he flicks on the light. "Time to get..." Charlie trails off. The bed that his brother sleeps in is empty. He shrugs his shoulders and heads down the hall to the bathroom.

*James isn't usually an early riser but there's a first time for everything.* "Hey Turd, you need to get ready for school," Charlie yells from the other side of the door. No response. He turns the knob and opens the door. Empty! *Well, where the hell is that little shit?*

Charlie heads back down the hallway but stops short when he passes the girls' room. "It's mine!" "No, it's mine!" Charlie hears the girls fighting over, more than likely, clothes! Those two love each other but they will draw blood over a piece of fabric.

"Hey you two, quit your fighting or you'll go to school in your underwear!"

"Not funny," Suzanne says.

"Yeah, not funny," Audrey repeats. The girls are like broken records. They always have to repeat the other.

# Avance

"I'm not being funny.  Knock it off and get dressed.  I mean it!"

Charlie closes their door and finishes his trip down the stairs.  The food smells good, far better than he could've possibly made.  He almost forgets about James when his stomach begins to rumble.  "Hey, have you guys seen James?"  He asks Clarissa and Charlotte.

"No, we haven't seen anyone but you, Charlie," Charlotte says while making googly eyes at him.

"Well, where in the hell can he be?"  Charlie questions no one in particular.

"Have you checked the bathroom?" Clarissa tries to help.

"Yeah, I've checked the bathroom and his bedroom.  His bed's been slept in but he's not there.  He's normally a late sleeper," Charlie explains.  "I'll look around outside.  Maybe he took the puppy outside."

"I saw the puppy in the laundry room.  I took her out just a few minutes ago," Charlotte explains.  "By the way, what's the puppy's name?"

"Her name is Ash.  With how crazy life has been, I'm surprised she's training as well as she is." Charlie nervously looks around for James as beads of sweat begin to form along his brow. *This is not what my father needs right now.*

*James has to be around here somewhere. I don't need to call my dad and inform him that, while mom is fighting for her life, James is missing and I have no clue where the hell he is.*

Clarissa removes the eggs from the pan and calls down for the girls. "Let me get the girls fed and then we will look for James together. How does that sound?"

"Yeah, okay. I'll be outside. Meet me when you're done." Charlie heads out. He's certain he won't be outside but you just never know.

Charlie begins searching all the places that he thinks James could be. He quickly strides to the old machine shed and looks around. "James?!" he yells out. Praying for a response he doesn't receive. "Damn it, where the hell are you?" Charlie mutters to himself before closing up the doors to the machine shed and heading to the barn.

He opens the barn doors. The stale smell of horse shit and hay prick his eyes. Since they took over the farm, he's cleaned out the barn and, without any animals, there hasn't been any contribution of excrements but the smell from the past still lingers. He knows that James wouldn't come in here but he still has to check it out before returning to the house. "James, are you in here?" He waits and listens—no response.

He closes the doors and runs back to the house.
Clarissa is adjusting her coat as she exits the
house. "Any sign of James?"

"No. I've checked both the machine shed and
the barn. He's not in either. I hate to say this,
but I think that we need to call the sheriff.
Something isn't right. James doesn't just take
off like this."

Clarissa wraps her arms around Charlie. "I think
you're right, Charlie. Let's get inside and give
the sheriff a call."

Chris hasn't had a decent night's sleep since
Scarlet was attacked. He's spent all his time at
the hospital. He hasn't even returned home to
shower. He's been depending on people to
bring him changes of clothes and the hospital
staff to allow use of the showers. His eyes are
blood shot and he has deep purple bags
surrounding them. His face has far more than a
five o'clock shadow.

"Hey Mr. Haggis," Alexander says from the
doorway to Scarlet's room. "How's she doing?"

Chris whips his head around but refuses to force
a smile. If Alexander had taken the threats
seriously when they were involved in the car
accident, maybe Scarlet wouldn't be lying in this
hospital bed. "You have any leads?"

"Not yet, but we did find a piece of evidence that is being processed for evidence right now. We should have a DNA profile within a few days," Alexander explains, trying to keep Chris in the loop. "Umm, but there's another reason I came here today. There's no easy way…"

"Quit pussy footing around and just spit it out already," Chris cuts Alexander off.

"James is missing."

Chris jumps from his seat and looks at Alexander like he had just grown two heads. "What the fuck do you mean James is missing? Where the fuck did he go?" Chris growls, menacingly. Just when he thought that things couldn't get worse, it did. First his wife is attacked and now his youngest son is missing.

"Well, Charlie got him down for bed last night but when he went to wake him for school this morning, he wasn't in bed. Charlie searched the house and the property and the state troopers are doing a detailed search for James now. I just thought you needed to be made aware of what was transpiring before you heard it on the news or from the town's folk."

"Great. Just fucking great. Now, what the hell am I supposed to do? Do I stay with my wife while one of my kids is missing or do I go home and leave my critically injured wife alone? This is just fucking great!" Chris starts to get loud.

# Avance

His heart is racing and he feels the urge to punch anything—or anyone.

"Chris, calm down. Look, there's nothing more you can do that we aren't already doing for James. Just stay near Scarlet. She'll need comfort when she wakes up and that comfort can only come from you," Alexander explains, putting a calming hand on Chris' shoulder.

"Yeah, that's easy for you to say. You're not in my shoes, now are you?"

Alexander feels lost for words. Nothing he can say or do will make Chris feel better. He can't even begin to imagine what he's feeling right now. "I'll keep you updated and I'll arrange to have the state troopers put someone at the hospital and your house to keep everyone else safe. This won't happen again."

# CHAPTER TWENTY-SEVEN

James wakes in an unfamiliar place. His head aches and his tummy hurts. He wants his mommy. "W-where am I?" James calls out to the mysterious figure across the room. The only light is the yellow flame of the fireplace in front of the dark figure. James feels vomit beginning to rise up his throat. Whatever was given to him to knock him out has made him ill. "Mister, I feel like I'm going to be sick," James pleads with the figure.

"Puke on the floor in front of you, just like the animal you are," the figure's voice boomed across the dark and desolate room. Not a speck of furniture sits in the room aside from a makeshift cot made out of old cloth and straw.

# Avance

"W-why am I here?" James questions as he fights the bile rising up his throat. The warm, watery taste that comes before vomiting is evident in his mouth.

"Why are you here? Why are you HERE?! I'll tell you why you're here. You're here because your mom didn't have the common sense to leave this town. You're here because your father is a monster; a monster that takes one child but leaves another. You're here because of them. Sorry about your luck, Pip Squeak, but you're my pawn now. Whether you make it out alive or not depends on the actions of your parents," the figure hisses at James. Shadows hide the figure's face but James's mind is racing. The figure looks familiar yet different somehow.

"I want my mommy," James begins to cry. His nerves are getting the best of him and he's unable to keep the bile at bay any longer. It rises quickly and sprays out his mouth.

"Look at this shit," the dark figure says before smacking James so hard that he's rendered unconscious.

***

Charlie is beside himself with grief and blame as troopers question him incisively about his activities the night before. When did he go to bed? What time did he see James last? Were there issues between him and his brother? He's getting tired of answering the same lame-ass questions and just wants his brother found. Who the hell could be doing this to his family? They haven't lived here long enough to have made enemies.

"Charlie?" A voice brings him out of his thoughts. "Would you like something to eat?" Clarissa questions, remorse seeping from her face.

"I couldn't eat right now, even if I wanted. I'm too nervous," Charlie's stomach does flip flops.

"I know this is a stressful time but if you don't eat you'll make yourself sicker than you already are," Clarissa has sympathetic eyes. "When you're ready to eat, I'll make you anything you want." She gently pats his shoulder and walks back inside the farm house leaving Charlie to his thoughts.

The night sky is full of twinkling stars. This is one of the many sights Charlie never got to experience living in Los Angeles. *Why the hell is someone hurting my family? I don't understand. We didn't do anything to them and we just want to live a peaceful existence and take in the beauty of this area. And now...now all of that has gone to hell in a hand basket.*

"Charlie," Alexander starts. "Is this James'?" He holds up a tattered old teddy bear.

# Avance

"That's Teddy Blue!" Charlie shouts out. "James would never, ever drop that thing and just leave it. It's his security blanket."

Alexander gets on his radio. "The bear is the boy's. Adjust the perimeter and spread out." Alexander draws his attention back to Charlie. "Do you know where James would have went over there?" Alexander points north of the property, out towards the second set of orchards that surround the farm.

"No! He wouldn't have left the property. We don't know anyone within walking distance and James is petrified of the dark. He never would've wandered alone." Charlie's fears and worries are washing over him like a thick flannel blanket.

"Ok son. We are expanding the perimeter. We will find your brother," Alexander reassures Charlie by his tone.

"But will you find him dead or alive?" Charlie questions. He asked a question that is surely on everyone's mind at this point. His fear that his brother may not come back alive is obvious in his thoughts. He had one job and that was to maintain the family unit so his father could stay at the hospital with his mother and he failed— miserably.

"Son, we will find him—alive. Whoever is doing this is out to scare your family, not kill them. I

am as sure as my next breath that he is alive
and we will get to him before you know it,"
Alexander places a hand on Charlie's shoulder,
trying to give him comfort but feeling that he's
failing at it.

# CHAPTER TWENTY-EIGHT

Alexander heads out with the state troopers searching the new, larger perimeter. Alexander takes off northeast of the farmhouse, searching high and low for James. His only thought, his only drive is to find that little boy safe and bring him home.

Alexander grew up in this town and he's been all over the countryside in the past three-plus decades but he's coming up on unfamiliar grounds. *I don't ever remember seeing this place before.* Alexander comes across a small stream with big oak trees on the other side of it.

With little thought, he jumps over the stream to investigate the little secret spot he's found. He slowly walks through the unfamiliar wooded area and comes to an opening. A small, run down shack sits across from him with smoke billowing from the fireplace. *That's odd. I've never known this place existed.* He slowly creeps to the shack under the cover of darkness.

Alexander peaks in and sees a roaring fire in the fireplace. He scans the room and notices a chair with a small figure sitting in it. Upon closer inspection, he realizes that the small figure is tied to the chair with his head hanging limp to his chest. *Fuck! No fucking way is this going on in my town.*

He reaches to radio for back up. No way can he enter in the shack without assistance. There's no telling how many perpetrators he's dealing with and he doesn't want to get the child killed while he tries to be the hero. He pushes the button and hears the crackle of static just seconds before a sharp pain shoots up his head and darkness begins to engulf him. "What the…"

Charlie paced the living room floor long enough. Too many hours were spent wearing holes in the carpet. Charlie knew that he could be of help to Alexander if only the stubborn, old Sheriff would let him. Not long after Alexander left—maybe five minutes—Charlie grabbed his coat and snuck out the back door while Clarissa and Charlotte were tending to the girls.

He had watched the direction that Alexander went and followed. He knew that he wasn't supposed to be doing this but he just couldn't sit around the house hoping and waiting. He needs to be out helping and searching. James was abducted; though, no one wants to use that word, while Charlie was in charge. This is his fault and his responsibility to help find his brother.

Alexander approaches a tree-infested area just a few yards off of the Haggis property. Charlie and his father hadn't fully explored the property so this is completely new to him. He slowly creeps up and over the stream. Charlie's careful to stay far enough back that Alexander doesn't see him yet close enough to make sure he doesn't lose him either.

Alexander creeps up to a house in the middle of all the large trees and peaks into the window. After a few quick heart beats, Charlie sees a dark shadow creeping up, quietly, behind Alexander. Before he can open his mouth to warn Alexander, the dark figure hits him over the head with a large rock.

The attacker laughs an evil laugh and hurries back inside the shack. *What the fuck is going*

*on? This is like something out of a horror movie. What the fuck am I supposed to do now?*
Charlie, as quietly as he crept into his hiding spot, creeps back out in search of help.

# CHAPTER TWENTY-NINE

"Great!  Just fucking great," the dark figured man paces back and forth in front of the fireplace. "You just couldn't stay the fuck away and leave me be, could you?  You had to come in search of the child and now..." he trails off.  "Now I have a big fucking mess on my hands."

Alexander is still knocked out and James is in a deep chloroform sleep.  The dark figure has to come up with a new plan and fast.  His rundown shack has been found and he can no longer stay here.  "Damn it," he screams as his fist comes into contact with the wooden walls.

He unties James and tosses him over his shoulder and begins to trek back toward the farm house. If he were a praying man, this would be the time that he would pray that no one sees him as he tries to sneak back into the enemy's compound. However, he isn't a man that believes in God. What God would create a man such as he? *This is fucking stupid. Going back and hiding in plain sight may be my undoing.*

As they approach their destination, he sulks lower to the ground and scopes out his surroundings. Not a light on inside the residence and only a lone porch light is illuminated. *Hot damn, I might be able to pull this off after all.* He tosses the kid on the ground and finishes scanning the property.

He lifts James up and finishes carrying him to the barn as quickly and quietly as possible. The kid may be small but lugging his dead weight more than half a mile would be tiring for the most in-shape person. "Fuck kid, you weigh more than a sack o' taters!"

He quietly opens the old barn door and drops James with a *thwack* on the dirt floor. He quickly, yet quietly, shuts the barn door and makes his way to the ladder that leads to the top of the old barn. He shimmies up the ladder, careful of each wooden rung, knowing that it could be rotted and unable to hold his weight.

# Avance

"Fuck, how am I supposed to get that damn kid up here?" he thinks when he reaches the top.

He stomps around the top of the barn, making sure it will hold his weight before he begins to pile up hay for James and him to rest on. *I can't believe that dumb old deputy botched my plans. I fucking hate winging shit. I'm literally on a wing and a prayer right now and nothing is fucking going as I had anticipated. This shit is getting old, and fast. I should've just fucking burned the house down when I had the chance and I wouldn't be running around like a chicken with its head cut off.*

He makes his way back down to where James lies, motionless. For good measure, he kicks James in the rib cage before grabbing him and tossing him over his shoulder. *This is fucking bullshit. I shouldn't have to carry this fucking repugnant boy up here.*

Just as he and James are settling down, a loud commotion comes from the old farm house. He rises from his positon and looks out a wide crack to see a shitload of state troopers gathering in front of the house with Charlie. "…And then he came up and bashed the deputy upside the head. He fell and the guy went back inside. I got scared and took off looking for help," he hears Charlie telling the troopers what he had done to the deputy that was snooping outside his shack.

"Fuck me," he thinks about the deputy lying on the cool, dark ground.  "Fuck, I hope I didn't leave anything behind that can tie this shit to me."

# CHAPTER THIRTY

Scarlet awakens with a horrific headache and pain shooting from her core to her side. "Ouch," she utters as she readjusts herself in a bed that is not hers.

"Hey baby, how're you feeling?" Chris is there, looking at the most gorgeous eyes he never thought he'd see again.

"I feel like…" she thinks a minute. *What the hell do I feel like?* "Like I was stabbed a few times," she tries to make light of what happened to her but Chris doesn't find it amusing in the slightest.

"Baby, this shit has gotten so far out of control.  I should have listened to you when you said that you wanted to go home—back to Los Angeles.  Baby, I swear, I swear on my parents' graves, that we will be packing up and heading back as soon as you recover.  I fucking promise," Chris curses.

"I'd like that," Scarlet rubs her hands through his hair.  She's been married to this man long enough to know that his eyes are weary and there's more going on than what meets the eyes.  "What's going on?"  Scarlet quizzically surveys Chris.

"Nothing, honey.  Nothing at all.  Just rest," Chris rises to kiss his wife on her forehead.

"Don't give me that nonsense," Scarlet becomes angry.  "You tell me what the hell is going on and you tell me right this minute, Chris!"  She stares him in the eyes, trying to keep her composure yet knowing she isn't doing a good job.

"Well, honey, it's just that…" he trails off, unable to find the words to tell his wife that their youngest son was taken from the home in the middle of the night almost twenty-four hours earlier.

"Chris, I'm really starting to get pissed off.  You better sp…"

# Avance

"James was taken from his bed last night," Chris blurts out, not really wanting to tell his wife like that.

"He what?" The words aren't registering to Scarlet. Her mind is racing a million miles a minute but the thought that someone has her baby boy doesn't seem to register. She can't seem to react in the appropriate manner for something like this. *Hell, is there even an appropriate manner for something like this?* "What the hell do you mean he was taken from his bed? Why the hell are you here and not out looking for our son?" She bellows, as she rises from her bed, ripping out her IV's and pulling off the EEG monitors from her head.

"Scarlet, baby, you need to lie back down. You have been out of it for days and had to have surgery. You're not well," Chris is trying to coax Scarlet back in bed as she runs around the room getting ready to…who knows what she's getting ready to do.

"Get your hands off me," she seethes when Chris encases her wrist in his hand. "This shit," she waves her hands in the air, "is all your fault. You did this to our family and then you sit in this hospital room, like the coward you are, instead of looking for our son." Scarlet pokes Chris' chest. Anger is an inappropriate word to describe what Scarlet is feeling; rage, hatred and wrath more describes the fury building within her very soul.

"Our son needed you," she continues. "But you, like the weakling you are, decided to stay by my bedside and what? Watch me sleep?" Her chest is heaving with every word she punches out. Her words, like daggers, slice through Chris' soul and his eyes show the hurt and pain they've caused, but Scarlet could give two-shits about how he feels.

A nurse races into the room when the alarms started sounding at the nursing station that alerted them to problems with their patient. "Mrs. Haggis, you need to get in bed right now. This isn't good for you or your healing process," the woman grabs her hand and tries to coax her to the bed.

"Get your fucking hands off me," Scarlet snarls, throwing the nurse back two steps as she pulls her arm away from her. "I'm going to find my son and God help you if you or anyone else tries to fucking stop me!"

Without another word, Scarlet throws on a pair of scrub pants under the gown she's wearing and storms out of the room. Not giving a rat's ass about her appearance, she passes the nurse station and straight the elevator. She taps her foot as she awaits the elevator's arrival to the fourth floor. "Scarlet," she hears Chris' voice come from behind her.

"Don't," she tosses her hand up, preventing Chris from finishing his sentence. "I don't want to hear about how I need to go back to my room and how I need to rest. You don't know what the fuck I need."

Chris hangs his head in shame. "I wasn't going to say that. I just…" he trails off not knowing how to say anything that won't make his wife ooze with antagonism.

"You just what?" The elevator doors open as Scarlet stares at Chris awaiting his reply.

"I just wanted you to wait up so I could drive you home. That's all. I know you don't understand what I was going through and I hope you never do, but I was torn. You weren't conscious and you were still on shaky ground when James went missing. I wanted to be there for him but I wanted to be with you too and I felt torn. I knew that the police had James' search under control so I decided to be with you when you woke up."

Foreboding and ferocity course through Scarlet's body. She begins to shake as her face turns a crimson color. "The police had his search under control? Are you fucking serious? Those pigs couldn't find their way out of a wet paper bag and you expect them to find our son? Did they ever find your parents' killer? Fuck no! Did they ever find who slashed our brake line? Nope! How about who shit all over my bed and fucking jizzed all over our girls' bed? That's right, I'm sure they haven't found him either. How you could be so naïve to believe that I would fall for some half-cocked lie from you is absolutely appalling," Scarlet walks into the elevator before she says anymore to Chris.

Hesitating for only a moment, Chris enters the elevator with Scarlet. The tension growing between them is thick. Scarlet's fuming and has a few more choice words for Chris but she keeps her mouth shut.

Chris turns to face Scarlet. "Hon…" He trails off when he sees her face. If he didn't know better, he would have been certain she was burning a hole into his head. He shuts his opened mouth and turns and faces the elevator doors.

# CHAPTER THIRTY-ONE

"Where's my son?" Scarlet screeches, running toward the group of troops huddled around her house. "Where is my baby at?"

"Ma'am," a young and very handsome State Trooper stops her by the shoulders. "We haven't found him yet but…"

"But what? You haven't found my son yet you're all outside of my house having a nice little break and shooting the fucking breeze," she rolls her eyes in disbelief before turning around to face Chris. "And you left the job of finding our son in the hands of these *fine* men," sarcasm rolls of her tongue like venom.

"God damn it, Scarlet," Chris fumes. "I'm sick and tired of this attitude bullshit. I've listen to you cut everyone down because no one is as fucking high and mighty in this damn town as your high class friends from Los Angeles. You know what, get over yourself and quit acting like such a bitch," Chris shakes as he takes in air into his lungs.

"I-I…" Scarlet trails off, unable to find the words that she needs to retort back to Chris.

"I-I, shut your mouth. I've heard enough from you tonight. I sat by your bedside and fucking prayed. I fucking prayed that you would survive and I was so happy when you woke up but that was short-lived. Once you started opening your mouth and judging everyone and everything around you, I wished—no, I prayed, that your mouth would quit working or that you would drift back into a coma."

Chris is clearly pissed and the troopers begin to fan out, extending and revising their search perimeter. Chris, without saying a word to Scarlet, walks into the house and slams the screen door behind him with such force that Scarlet jumps at the sound. *What an asshole,* the thought crosses her mind and she knows, without a shadow of a doubt, that she is falling out of love with the man that she, so many years ago, vowed to love through the good and bad times. When she made that vow, however, she never expected that one of their bad times would destroy them indefinitely.

She kicks a dirt clod and moves toward the south, away from the farm house and near to the barn and machine shed. She can't face her husband right now and she definitely wants nothing at all to do with that evil fucking house! She regrets the day she agreed to move to this fucking place. She used to be such a happy and carefree woman but since moving here, she's become angry and venomous toward her husband.

"Scarlet," she hears her name from behind her. She whips around.

"Alexander, what happened to your head?" She's curious seeing him standing there with an ice pack on the back of his head.

"Oh, nothing, just a little bump," blushing as he nonchalantly shakes off his injury. "Hey, I just wanted to let you know that James is still alive. I saw him but I couldn't get to him. He's still in the area and we are searching with every tool we have to bring him home."

Scarlet's eyes widen in disbelief. *Alexander saw my baby but didn't get him? How could this be? How can an officer just see a missing child and not get him—bring him home.* She feels a burning in her core as anger begins to fill every nerve ending in her body. "What the fuck do you mean you saw him but you didn't bring him home? What the hell happened? Aren't you supposed to be the law—to serve and protect? You have failed this family on a number of occasions. How the fuck you're still an officer boggles my mind!"

Scarlet can't tolerate to look at the deputy any longer. Repulsion and hostility are the only emotions that she can even conjure up toward Alexander. She turns on her heals and continues to saunter toward the end of the property, where the old barn sits. At least in the old barn she'll get the peace she so desperately longs for; the peace in which to cry and scream and yell without people around to hassle her.

She makes her way into the old barn and, by the light of the moon; she finds an old lantern hanging on the wall with a box of matches. *Maybe, just maybe there's enough kerosene in the lamp to burn for a few hours,* she thinks. She grabs the lantern and begins fumbling with it to get it to light.

"Ha, there we go." The light from the lantern illuminates the barn. She holds it out in front of her and begins to sweep around the barn, checking everything out. She'd never been in here before and she can see why. There's not a damn thing inside of it and it's in dire need of repair.

## Avance

The lantern lights up the final half of the room when she catches something out of the corner of her eye. She quickly positions the lantern in the direction of the movement. Her breath hitches as she comes face to face with the person who'd been stalking her and her family. "W-who are you?" Fear rushes through her as her eyes lock with, what words can only describe as Satan himself.

# CHAPTER THIRTY-TWO

"Hello, Scarlet," the deep voice groans as he takes one and then two steps toward the woman who is shaking in her boots. "I'm a little surprised to see you're still around. I thought you would've gotten the message to get the hell outta here long ago but you didn't. I'm rather disappointed in you." He shakes his head.

"I-I wanted to leave. I did, but my husband—Chris, wouldn't. I want to leave now and I will, but I can't leave until I find my son. Once I get James back, I'll pack myself and my family up and I'll leave. I promise, just please give me my child back." Scarlet trembles with fear as she struggles to keep her bile down.

# Avance

"I'm sorry. No can do sista! He's mine now. If you cared about him like you claim you do, you should've left and never looked back months ago. He's mine now, as is the rest of the family. You, however, you're disposable. I don't need, nor do I want you. So, now it's your time to die, just like the old fuckers I slaughtered." His eyes dance with excitement. The eyes are the pathway to the soul and, in this instance; Scarlet knows this kid has no soul.

"Mary Ellen and Carl? You killed them? But...but I don't understand why? Why would you kill them and then torture and stalk my family and then..." Scarlet can't even finish the sentence. It's too horrific to think that this kid—whoever he is, is going to kill her next. She looks around the barn trying to find any way out.

"Yep! I sure did. I slid that knife right across that old bitch's throat and watched the life drain out of her face. I shot the old man in his knee cap. Oh the sound he made warmed me to the core. When he begged me, and oh he begged, it brought a smile to my face. I was in control of whether he lived or died and I had already chosen his fate.

"I killed both of them right there in the house that you and your husband so comfortingly sleep in. It wasn't too much work though," he twirls the tip of a knife on his thumb. "You see, they were sticklers for routine. I just observed them for a few days, learned their routine and then attacked when they were the most vulnerable." A slight smile forms along his face.

Scarlet knows that he's replaying their slaughter in his mind and is completely repulsed by it. Her stomach heaves as bile erupts out of her mouth; forceful and quick. There was no stopping the bile from exiting her body, no matter how hard she tried. Her stomach retches with dry heaves before she's able to regain her bearings and try to talk her way out of this—her certain death. "Why are you doing this to my family? What have we ever done to you?"

Anger flickers in his eyes before he moves, quickly, toward Scarlet. "What the fuck did you do to me?" His tone, fuming with hatred and wrath, causes Scarlet to jump. "I'll tell you what your fucking *family* did to me. They fucking abandoned me!" He huffs in, heavily, every bit of air he can suck in. "They threw me away like I was a fucking piece of garbage. Their own flesh and blood, tossed to the wolves like a rotten piece of meat!"

"Family? Threw you away?" Scarlet's brain is unable to comprehend just what the fuck is going on here. She was under the impression that Chris was the only living relative. "I'm sorry, I don't understand."

# Avance

"What?  Did Chris just fail to mention his sister?
The children that she bore?  Come on, I'm not
fucking stupid so quit playing the innocent little
bitch!"  He stares at her while his face contorts
to something more evil and sinister.

"Marie?  You're Marie's son?"  Scarlet's
eyebrows fall downward as confusion sweeps
over her more than understanding.

"Marie?"  The confusion that Scarlet has is now
transferring to him.  "Her name was fucking
Laura!"  He yells as his body shakes and spittle
flies.

"Laura?  But…but Laura is Charlie's mom and
Chris' ex-girlfriend…" then realization hits her.
"You…no, this can't be right," tears perforate her
eyes.

"Now the lights are coming on," his evil smile
returns.  He's finding too much bliss in torturing
Scarlet with the Haggis family secrets.

"But…but that's…"  She trails off, unable to find
the right words.

"And do you know who my father is?  Would you
like to take a guess?"  He looks at Scarlet but,
she's no longer participating.  Her mind is still
reeling from what she's learned.  "Come on,
Scarlet.  Just take a guess."

# CHAPTER THIRTY-THREE

"Chris!" He yells at Scarlet. "Chris is my fucking father."

Scarlet is taken aback. She's trying to wrap the news around her head. *If Laura was his sister, then how in the hell is he the father?* Then it hits her all at once. Her mouth drops in complete horror at what transpired here before she met Chris. She feels her stomach begin to knot as bile threatens to vacate her body again.

"That's right!" He says realizing that Scarlet is now seeing the full picture. "Chris is both my uncle and my dad. I suppose that makes his sister both my mom and my aunt," he ponders that for just a moment.

"But...that's just so..." Scarlet has no words to say. She can't even think straight. She feels as if the breath has been sucked out of her lungs and she's struggling to breathe.

"Nasty? Disgusting? Gross? Or, hey, I've heard this one a lot...an abomination?" He helps her find the words that she's struggling to find, the words that are evading her.

"But, then who does Charlie belong to?" So many questions flood her mind.

"Oh, the twisted tale gets even better. That cold December night, two children were born to the sick and twisted siblings. They had a set of identical twin boys. Boys who would be named Charles and Benjamin. As you've probably guessed already, I'm Benjamin but I go by Ben," he says with the evil smile creeping back on his face.

Scarlet begins to hyperventilate with all the disturbing revelations being thrown at her. The man she married and thought she had known for nearly two decades was not who she thought. He was a mess and committed...incest! "But, why? Why did he leave you but take Charlie?"

He shrugs. "Hell if I know. Maybe it was the fact that I was deformed. I was born with some deformities that I had fixed along the way in foster care. I guess I just wasn't the perfect boy for Chris to love."

Scarlet knows that that question struck a nerve with Ben. He'd been abandoned and he doesn't know why. One child was chosen over the other and it bothers him profusely. If she continues to pry, one of two things could occur. Ben could go off the deep end and snap or he could break down. Scarlet chooses that the former would probably be the way he would go so she leaves it be—for now. "What happened to Laura?"

"Laura. Hmm, well after Chris left her and took Charlie, well she never recovered from it. She had me, but I wasn't fucking enough for her. I was the fucked up kid and, six months after Chris left her, she hung herself. Right here in this very barn." He waves his hands around for effect. "Not long after her suicide, the old fucker and his wife got rid of me. Put me up for adoption but no one wanted a deformed baby. What was it that they called me...Oh, that's right, *retard*."

Scarlet is reeling from all of this. This is far too much for her to grasp in such a small amount of time. *Why did I storm away from the house? How long until someone comes searching for me?* Her body begins to fail her as tears start to stream down her cheeks. *This can't be fucking happening. This is all a bad dream. It has to be!*

"Quit your fucking crying!" Ben snaps; his fists enclosed ready to strike Scarlet for the tears. "Crying doesn't get you anywhere and I know that those tears aren't for me so stop!" His lips purse and his eyes slant.

Scarlet regains her composure and stops the tears from falling, though it's one of the hardest things she's had to do. "Ben, I'm sorry about what happened to you, I really am. I had no idea that Chris had another son or what he had done with his sister. I swear, I'm as much a victim in all of this as you are. Please, you have to believe me. You need to let me go." Scarlet begs for her life. She's being punished for her husband's sins.

"I don't have to do anything I don't want to do," Ben retorts. "No one has done a damn thing for me so why should I do you any favors?"

"Ben, I know that you were treated unjustly and it wasn't fair but you have to understand, I didn't do anything to you. I didn't even know you existed. The person that you're angry with is Chris. You need to tell him how you feel and take your frustrations out on him," Scarlet tries to defuse the situation. She's grasping at straws to try to get out of this alive.

"Mom?" James calls from the top of the barn. Scarlet cranes her head up and sees her sweet little boy looking down at her, groggy and ill. "Mom, I don't feel so good," James warns before vomit spews from his mouth, off the side of the flooring and right on to Ben.

Ben, in pure disgust, begins to shout. "What the fuck? You did that shit on purpose!" He turns to head back to James. Anger radiates from his body and Scarlet knows that her youngest son is in danger.

Scarlet reaches after Ben and pulls his arm. "Stay away from my son!" With strength she didn't realize she possessed, she throws Ben back. He falls to the ground knocking over the lantern. The kerosene spills along the remaining hay in the barn and, before either can act, the barn floor is engulfed in flames.

"Look what you did!" Ben yells as he begins to race to the doors, exiting the burning inferno. He throws the door open and is face to face with Alexander. With a swing of his fist, he strikes Alexander in the jaw and tries to push past him. "Get out of my way!"

Bill, from the state police, comes up and wraps his arm around Ben and brings him crashing to the floor with a loud thud. "You're under arrest," Bill explains as he wrestles with the suspect, trying to cuff his hands.

# Avance

"Get off me you fucking pig." Ben continues to wrestle with Bill as Scarlet moves on up the ladder to reach James. Her heart races and sweat forms down her spine as the fire warms her. She knows that she's in danger but she needs to get to her son before she can flee to safety.

"Mommy's coming for you, James. Just hold on," she comforts him as sobs fill the barn between the crackling and popping of burning wood. Just as she places her hands on the floor of the second floor, the ladder wrung breaks and she's left hanging on for her own life.

The ladder crashes to the ground with a loud *thud* and Scarlet struggles with all her might to pull herself up to her son. The pain in her side is excruciating as the stitches that hold her wounded skin together begin to tear and pull. "Ahahah, fuck!" Scarlet yells at the burning pain. She holds on for dear life and, with all she has, pulls herself up and to her son. "It's okay, James. Mommy's here." She strokes his head and kisses his cheek.

"Scarlet?!" Chris hollers as he barrels in the barn, jumping over Alexander, Bill and Ben. He doesn't even take notice at who the men are arresting. Scarlet's scream is why he's here. "Scarlet, where are you?"

"Up here, Chris!" His eyes dart to the top of the barn where Scarlet and James are huddled together. "Hang on! I'll get you down." The fire's burning wildly out of control. Chris searches all around trying to find a way to climb up to them. "I'll be back," he explains as he races out of the barn.

Bill is dragging Ben out and placing him in a patrol car while Alexander is rubbing his swollen lip when Chris races past them. "What are you doing?" Alexander looks at Chris with confusion and bewilderment.

"I'm trying to save my family!" He says just seconds before the roof collapses and he hears high-pitched screams coming from Scarlet and James. His heart races as thoughts of burying his wife and son wash over him.

# CHAPTER THIRTY-FOUR

Chris looks at the barn, lying in shambles in front of him. Some troopers are racing with water hoses and he hears the faint sound of sirens down the road but it's too late; too late to save his family. Chris' heart races as he sees his life burn before him. His wife, his youngest son—gone forever. His knees hit the ground as Alexander rushes to his side.

"What the fuck did I do to deserve this?" Chris throws his hands up toward the Heavens. "Tell me! What the fuck did I do?" Sobs escape his mouth as his chest rattles and his body quivers.

Alexander, not knowing what else to do, places a hand upon Chris' shoulders. No words are exchanged, no comfort given, just a silent prayer for Scarlet and little James.

Chris looks back to the old barn and sees the ruins of old, flame-engulfed wood move and a light cough. "They…they're still alive!" He shouts as he rises to his feet and runs toward the pile. "I'm coming!"

Alexander is hot on his heels. The two men bend down and begin pulling smoldering wood away. They don't care that the wood is burning their hands or that the smoke is irritating their lungs. "Help!" Alexander yells to get the attention of the officers. "They're still alive."

All the officers race to the other side of the burning barn and, with bare hands, begin moving and throwing things to get to Scarlet and James. "Can you hear me?" Chris screams as he throws burning wood to the side. He reaches in and finds a small hand. "I have James!" Chris pulls his lifeless son from the rubble. His face is covered in soot and his breathing is shallow and irregular.

The fire engine pulls down the dirt road and cuts the sirens. Five firefighters race out and begin to ready the hose to battle the flames. "My wife…she's still in there," he warns as he begins to compress James's chest.

# Avance

Four of the firefighters rush to the rubble to assist the officers whilst one fighter races to James to assist Chris. "His breathing…it's just not right!" Chris states, anxiety riddling his body.

"Sir, I'll take it from here. Go to the end of the driveway and flag down the paramedics when they arrive." The firefighter takes over care of James as Chris races down the driveway. Chris halts his movements as he passes a patrol car that held the person responsible for all of this— for the fire and the stalking and the injuries to his family. Without thinking, without awareness, Chris opens the door to the patrol car and rips the individual from the back seat.

"You! Why the fuck did you…" he's taken aback. He's looking at the face of his son, Charlie, but different. The face isn't exactly Charlie, but it's close enough to make Chris stutter and stop mid-sentence. "But…how? Why?"

An evil laugh sounds through the night air; above the crackling of the fire and the sounds of the fire trucks rumbling engine. "Why not? You abandoned me. You picked one over the other. You left me and never looked back." The smile turns to something evil—scary. "Did you really think you could move back here; to the place where you fucked my mom—your sister, and go about living a happy, normal life with your new family?"

"What?" Chris shakes his head. "You were left with your mom. I couldn't take care of two kids. It wouldn't have been fair to you or Charlie! Ben, why are you doing this shit to my family?"

"Oh, you do remember my fucking name. Yippy," he smiles sadistically while speaking in a sarcastic tone. "Would you like a Father-of-the-Year award?"

"God dammit, Ben! This isn't a fucking game. I left you with your mom and grandparents. I didn't know Laura was going to commit suicide," Chris screams.

"Dad?" Charlie's voice echoes behind Chris. "What in the hell is going on?" His eyes move between the fire at the barn and his father.

"Son, it's alright. Go back inside," Chris glances over his shoulder at the son he's raised since the minute he was born.

"Does he even know about me?" Ben questions, evil radiating from his eyes.

"Don't. You leave him be!"

"Know about who?" Charlie walks up. He takes a look at the man in cuffs and staggers back. "Dad, what's going on?" He takes in the face, his face, staring back at him. The kid in cuffs looks just like him yet slightly different.

# Avance

"Hey, look, it's my *older* brother," Ben laughs as he stares at Charlie. "How ya doin' bro?"

"That's enough," Chris growls, anger doesn't even describe what he's feeling.

"What's going on, Dad?" Charlie is growing restless. Chris knows he needs some answers but he's at a loss for words. He just stares at his boy, racking his brain for the right thing to say but how do you tell someone that they are a product of incest and, oh by the way, you also have twin brother whom I decided not to take with me when I left?

"Where to begin?" Ben starts, clearly taking control of the situation. "You see, Daddy over here was so *in love* with his own sister that he couldn't keep his dick dry around her..."

"Shut the fuck up!" Chris is steaming mad. He hates the predicament that Ben has forced him into and he damn sure wasn't going to allow him to tell Charlie the story behind his birth. "Look son," he faces Charlie. "When I was eighteen, I did some stupid shit. I fell in love with my sister, Laura, and we couldn't fight the urge to be with each other. I was stupid but I just couldn't help it.

"We had sex and eventually, we created you and your twin brother, Ben," he looks toward Ben and back to Charlie. "When you boys were born, my dad was livid. He knew immediately that I had fathered you two and he kicked me out. I grabbed you and I left that night and never looked back."

"I fucking knew it," Alexander pipes in, overhearing the conversation between father and son. "I fucking knew that you and your sister were doing shit that you weren't supposed to be doing but no one fucking believed my theory."

"Alexander, this doesn't concern you," Chris glares at the deputy. "This is a family affair and I suggest you get out of it."

"To hell it doesn't concern me. I, as well as many troopers, injured ourselves rescuing your wife and son from a fire that your illegitimate twin son that you created with your sister started because of some stupid ass shit that you did." Alexander's eyes narrow. "And, to make matters worse, this shit could've been solved a long ass fucking time ago with little injuries if you just would've told us what you did. You risked so many lives all because you were ashamed of something you did more than fifteen years ago— and you rightfully should be ashamed!"

Chris ignores Alexander and looks back at Charlie. "I don't know what happened after I left Nebraska. Ben and Laura were supposed to live their lives as they saw fit but Laura...well she killed herself just six months later." Chris catches his breath. "Our relationship began in that old barn," he points toward the barn that now lies in rumble. "And her life ended in that barn."

"And now, if I get my way, your new wife's life will end in that barn too." Ben laughs his evil laugh before Alexander snatches him and tosses him back in the patrol car, slamming the door with such force that the entire cruiser shakes side to side.

Chris hangs his head in shame. Shame has always eaten at him over the years but it was shame that he could keep hidden. Now that his secret was out, there was more shame and embarrassment riddling his body.

Alexander finds some remorse for what Chris has been through. He doesn't agree with what he's done but it's in the past. "Hey man," Alexander breaks Chris' train of thought. "Scarlet was found and is alive. She's being taken to the hospital as well as James for observation. That's what I came over here for before I overheard your conversation with that dumb fuck," Alexander nods his head to the cruiser.

"Look, I don't know what to say or if I should say anything at all. What happened in the past is just that; the past. Is what you did right? No, not in the slightest, but don't let that shit haunt you anymore. You have a great family here and, yes you did some fucked up shit when you were a kid, but who hasn't?" Alexander pats Chris on the shoulder and gives him a ragged smile before walking back to the rest of the emergency crew.

Chris sighs and runs his fingers through his hair. *This has turned into a huge fucking mistake!* He turns back toward Charlie and sees confusion sweeping over the boy's face. "Son," Chris begins. "I'm sorry that all of this came to a head the way it has."

Charlie throws his hand up. "Just stop. I think you've done enough damage tonight. In fact, I'm disgusted. I'm a fucking disgrace! I was created out of incest; a fucking sick ass scandal! You are a sick man, Dad, or maybe I should call you Uncle Chris since it seems that you are both my uncle and my dad!" Charlie turns and storms back in the house leaving Chris to his own, twisted thoughts.

Chris turns to Ben. "Why? Why the fuck would you do this? What the fuck happened to you?" Chris seethes with anger and upheaval.

"Why?" Ben looks him dead in the face with nothing but anger and hatred building up behind his eyes. "Why you fucking ask? I did it because of what your fucking choice did to me. The abuse that I suffered at the hands of the parents the state put me with. The abuse I suffered from the other children because I was fucking different. I was only different because of the fucked up shit you did with your own damn sister."

Alexander walks up to Chris and places his hand on his shoulder. "Come on, he's not worth it. All he's doing is saying shit to piss you off and it's working. Let's get you to the hospital with your wife and son."

Chris gives Ben one more look. He looks like Charlie but the darkness and callousness behind his eyes is nothing like Charlie. Ben is pure evil and maybe, just maybe, the spawn of Satan himself. Surely, this was the punishment that God inflicted upon Chris for the transgression that he committed with his sister.

# EPILOGUE

### ★★★10 years later★★★

The fire and the spilling of his secrets left Chris without a family.  Scarlet and James were hospitalized for nearly a week with first and second degree burns and smoke inhalation. Ben was arrested and charged with several counts of attempted murder and mayhem as well as two counts of murder and would spend the rest of his natural life behind prison walls.

James suffered from smoke inhalation and burns covering twenty percent of his body.  He was in the burn unit for a little more than a week before he was released.  James has no idea what exactly transpired but had a lot of questions—questions that Chris didn't answer.

Scarlet was in the hospital for several weeks. She was burned over sixty percent of her body. She had to have skin grafts and her life was touch and go early on. The last time Chris saw her, she was wrapped in sterile gauze and screaming at him to "get the fuck out" so he left and never turned back around.

When Scarlet was released, she immediately told Chris that they were over and that she would be filing for divorce as soon as she reached Los Angeles. Chris' world was shattered. He had loved Scarlet almost as much as he had loved Laura and now she was gone forever. Chris had done some fucked up shit in his life but he felt that the past should remain there. No one should be judged on things that they did in the past. Everyone has a past and the past is what lays the groundwork for their future.

Last he heard, Scarlet had moved on with her life and retained her old job. Furthermore, she was engaged to a handsome man that made six figures a year. He knew all about her past and everything that had happened to her and accepted her for who she is.

Charlie decided that he wanted to live with Scarlet because he just couldn't trust Chris anymore. The bond that he and his son once shared was broken, permanently damaged with no chance of repair. It was probably for the best since Chris could no longer look into Charlie's eyes without seeing all the mistakes he'd made over the years. Charlie went on to graduate high school in the top of his class and won a full scholarship to UCLA and had majored in criminal justice and was now a police officer.

Ben was sentenced to life in prison for the murders against his grandparents. The district attorney decided not to prosecute him for the crimes against Chris and his family because it wouldn't have done any good since Ben will never see the light of day again. Since there was no trial because Ben struck a plea deal saving him from a death sentence, no one knew all of his history. But it was discovered that Ben had been physically and sexually abused in, at least, one foster home.

"Chris," a voice calls him back. "It's time to go." Eva, his new wife, was a blessing in disguise. After the sale of the property in Greenwich and the divorce was settled, Chris moved to Iowa and bought a small farmhouse with a decent amount of land. It was here that he met Eva; the beautiful daughter of a wealthy farmer. They married within a year and started a family of their own shortly after.

"Coming honey," he walks out, after putting Ash in the pen out back, and meets up with his new wife and their three children; Joseph, Samuel and baby Bethany. Eva knows nothing of his past and never will, if he has his say on the matter. With the divorce and custody, he signed away his rights to the kids and a clause was added that, at no time, will any of the Haggis children from Scarlet or Laura go in search of Chris. The past should remain just that, the past, and should never be allowed into the present.

The End

# AUTHOR'S NOTE

Thank you for reading Twisted Destiny.
Project E-X2 will release mid-2016. Check
my webpage for updates.
www.veavance.com. Also, follow me on
facebook for giveaways and advanced
readers copies of upcoming releases.
www.facebook.com/VEAvance